OTHER
Harlequin Romances
by ROSE ELVER

1949—SHINING WANDERER

Many of these titles are available at your local bookseller
or through the Harlequin Reader Service.

For a free catalogue listing all available Harlequin Romances,
send your name and address to:

HARLEQUIN READER SERVICE,
M.P.O. Box 707, Niagara Falls, N.Y. 14302
Canadian address: Stratford, Ontario, Canada   N5A 6W4

Fire Mountain

by

ROSE ELVER

Harlequin Books

TORONTO • LONDON • NEW YORK • AMSTERDAM • SYDNEY • WINNIPEG

Original hardcover edition published in 1976
by Mills & Boon Limited

ISBN 0-373-02054-6

Harlequin edition published March 1977

Printed in U.S.A.

CHAPTER ONE

'WILL you marry me, Amelia?'

Amelia was so startled she almost dropped the pencil she had been meticulously sharpening while the professor sipped his coffee and brooded over his notes. He had been fidgeting with his papers for the last ten minutes, and she had supposed that his mind was miles away, probably on the jungle slopes of the volcanic island of Sarava, preoccupied with some absorbing detail of his researches there.

But this proposal, coming like a bolt from the blue, was so incredibly unlikely and unexpected that she sat gripping the pencil and staring at him, her eyes wide and blank behind her horn-rimmed spectacles.

'Sorry! I rather slung that at you, didn't I!' He set down his coffee cup with a clatter, swivelled round in his chair and went over to the long, low windows of the cottage which looked out across a stretch of lawn to the haphazard cluster of apple trees laden with blossom at the bottom of the small garden.

There he stood, his back to her. He seemed very remote; a tall, spare figure, impressive even in his fisherman's-knit sweater and worn slacks. The light from the window traced threads of silver in his thick, dark hair and outlined the strong bone structure of his angular profile.

Amelia's deep, secret love for this man swept over

her like pain. She closed her eyes for a second against it and the pencil snapped in two under the pressure of her fingers.

At the small, sharp click he turned round. 'Does it sound such an outlandish proposition?'

Flinging himself into his chair again, he pushed the papers and coffee cup aside and lit a cigarette. His knuckles shone white against the flare of the lighter, and in that small gesture revealed his complex character—the dominant will controlling the inner tensions of the highly-strung.

For the moment the atmosphere in the room was strained, so extraordinary as to be almost dreamlike. Wordless still, Amelia poked the sensible round spectacles, that would keep slipping down her nose, back into position with a shaky forefinger. She brushed the fragments of pencil lead from her shabby skirt.

It took her another full minute to say, as sedately as she could: 'I don't think I understand, Professor.'

'What is there to understand?' He blew an impatient wreath of smoke. 'I've asked you to be my wife, and if we can discuss it reasonably for a few minutes now it may help you to come to a decision.'

'Are you serious?'

'Perfectly serious.'

She looked up at last to meet the grey eyes intent on her. They were grave and thoughtful, and it was an effort to keep her composure, for her brain refused to accept any of this as reality.

Yet it was real enough; the long, familiar room at the back of the cottage, flooded with afternoon sunlight; white plastered walls and old oak beams,

6

polished boards underfoot with a long threadbare rug, the lumpy, chintzy armchair in the corner; the desk, strewn with notebooks and piles of typescript and blow-up photo stills from the films he had taken; her own rickety table, a makeshift for the portable typewriter; even the few sprays of apple blossom she had cut that very morning from some of the lower branches and arranged in a blue china bowl on the window sill.

And the man himself was only too real. A distinguished anthropologist with a bold, incisive mind who could be so coolly austere at times and at others so tense and restless. Donovan Lyne, for whom her love had gradually grown in the agonizing knowledge that it was hopeless and must be hidden not only from him but from the knowing glances and suppressed laughter of others. This man who must have known many beautiful, accomplished women.

'How long have you worked for me, Amelia?'

'A year ... I remember, the blossom had just come out on those trees.'

'Time enough to rub off the edges of acquaintanceship and get to know one another, would you say?' He drew on the cigarette. 'You agree we're compatible?'

'Well, yes, I suppose so,' she said cautiously.

'Let me put my own position to you first. When I came back from the expedition to Sarava I'd picked up a type of jungle fever, and I needed time to recuperate and to get my notebooks and photographic material into some kind of order in preparation for the book. I took indefinite leave from the Foundation and hired this cottage. Peace and quiet, with time to relax and get fit and put my ideas together. When I began to feel well enough to cope with some preliminary work on the book, my department offered to send a stenographer down. I was asking Mrs Maggs about the possibility of accommodation in Whimpleford, and quite gratuitously she suggested I needn't bother as you would probably fill the bill better than anybody from town.'

'Mrs Maggs!' Amelia was surprised to learn at this late stage that the stout, kindly woman who came in to cook and clean for the professor, and whose husband owned the cottage, had had a hand in her being here.

'A perspicacious old girl, our Mrs Maggs,' he stubbed out the cigarette. 'I might as well admit that I then made a point of getting to know your brother-in-law for the specific purpose of meeting you and looking you over.'

'I see,' she said warily, her cheeks reddening slightly.

'Does the idea offend you?' His smile glinted briefly. 'No reason why it should. I kept very much to myself the first couple of months I was here, and I couldn't imagine a village like this coming up with the kind of secretary-cum-assistant I required. On the other hand, I wasn't too keen on importing a town-bird who would get bored with the life I lead and go hopping off in a car for the bright lights at any and every opportunity.' Running his fingers through his thick hair, he went on: 'It was an outside chance, but it paid off. Country-bred girl, college education, intelligent and sensible, and competent with a type-writer. The fact that you'd actually been studying anthropology was too good to be true. You've been a godsend, my dear girl.'

She said in a level voice: 'I've enjoyed it too, Professor.'

Donovan Lyne's eyes narrowed. 'I'm glad.' He looked away and then back to her. 'You've become indispensable to me, Amelia.'

Her heart turned over, but she continued to watch him calmly, saying nothing in return. Indispensable? —yes, like a comfortable coat in winter.

He stirred restlessly and rubbed the back of his neck, flexing his shoulders. 'I have to go back to London soon, and pick up my life, and I want you to come with me. You're out of your element here with your sister and brother-in-law, and to be brutal, I don't see that they have any obligation to provide you with a home.'

'Nor have you!' she retorted more sharply than she realised. 'After all, Whimpleford *is* my home.'

'Face up to it,' he insisted brusquely, 'you're not happy with them. Before you took this job with me you were merely trying to justify your existence by doing any odd jobs they chose to foist on you. They've managed for a whole year without you, and I would judge from your sister's temperament that she would prefer not to have you under her feet all the time again.'

This time she had to make a tremendous effort not to reveal her mortification by answering bitterly.

He was right. Of the two sisters, Emma had always

9

been the beautiful one, with a confident charm neither their parents nor anyone else could ever resist. Amelia had had the dubious consolation of a serene, practical outlook which had helped her, from a very early age, to come to terms with the fact that it was no use trying to compete with Emma's extrovert personality. So she had quietly withdrawn from Emma's clique, and become absorbed in her studies and her own interests to the point where she was completely indifferent to outward appearances.

'Oh, for heaven's sake, Melly!' Emma would comment furiously. 'You're no beauty, but there's no need for you to be such a drag. Thousands of plain-looking women project themselves through their clothes and personalities, but you're so *negative*. I daren't introduce you to my crowd because you always manage to look like a jumble sale. And that dreary, bookish chitchat drives the men a mile off.'

Amelia had laughed off these attacks with an equanimity which never failed to exasperate Emma; but it had distressed her mother, whose affectionate attempts to change Amelia's style and bring her out of her shell had never succeeded. Only her father had seemed to understand that her attitude was a refuge behind which Amelia was determined to build an independent life to satisfy and fulfil herself.

Some of Emma's sallies had penetrated, leaving scars of hidden hurt, and it was almost a relief when Amelia left home to go to university. Meanwhile Emma had become engaged to the handsome, wealthy sportsman who had bought the old Manor

House estate and turned it into an expensive and very exclusive country club. Amelia had submitted to being dressed up for the wedding, but had retreated as soon as possible to the familiar, congenial background of like minds at her college.

Then, a few months before she could take her degree, her parents were involved in a pile-up on a motorway, her mother killed and her father cruelly maimed. Amelia could think of nothing but her beloved father in need, and gave up her studies to return home and nurse him for two pain-filled years.

It was Emma and her businesslike husband, Edward, who had taken over the running of the family's prosperous market garden, leaving Amelia to cope with the invalid. And when he had died, Emma had decreed that Amelia move into a small room at the back of the club until she had decided what to do with herself.

Feeling tired and bereft, Amelia could not make up her mind whether to try to return to her studies and take up where she had left off, or look around for some kind of job, but her pride would not allow her to live off her sister. For the time being she had insisted on looking after Emma's rather spoilt twins, doing some clerical work in the office of the country club, and learning to use the typewriter with the vague notion that it would be useful whatever she might decide to do once she could rouse herself from the weight of mourning and inertia. She was conscious of the fact that most of the sophisticated members of the club looked on her as a rather

11

amusing oddity; many were not even aware that she was Emma's sister, but thought her the children's nanny. But the most difficult of her problems was the knowledge that Emma was finding her presence increasingly irritating and that Edward was inclined to become more and more patronising towards her as the weeks dragged by.

It was at this crucial point that the solution had come, without any effort on her part. The distinguished Professor Donovan Lyne, whose work on the Fire Mountain of Sarava had been featured in magazines and on television, and who had been living like a hermit crab in one of the cottages the other side of the village repelling all overtures from the locals to get to know him, had turned up at the country club one day and surprisingly become a member. Edward was extremely flattered and made good use of his name among the members; Emma, a keen celebrity-hunter, was thrilled at first but later pronounced him rather a cold fish and very stand-offish. Amelia, who had longed to meet him and perhaps have an opportunity of asking about his work, tried to screw up her courage once or twice to go into the club lounge, but was hastily and pointedly given something else to do by her sister. The club was for relaxation, not for the family frump to monopolize one of the important guests and badger him about his work.

They just happened to meet—or so Amelia had thought—in the grounds of the Manor House estate when she was returning with the children after an evening walk and Professor Lyne was taking a short cut back to his cottage. They fell into conversation; a tentative and yet curiously stimulating conversation which had resulted in an invitation to her to visit the cottage the following week, to look at some of his material and continue the discussion over one of Mrs Maggs's ample teas. A week later she was working for him, much to Emma's chagrin, for after that his visits to the country club had virtually ceased.

Mrs Maggs—*deus ex machina!* The plump personification of providence, Amelia thought wryly. She could almost hear the old woman's well-meaning recommendation: 'No sense in getting one o' they flibberty-gibberties from town. That there Miss 'Melia, now, sister of Mrs Denton of the Manor House club, wastin' her time she is. She would do for you, sir, bein' as she's book-learned, and not much else for the likes of her here now that her father's gone, poor soul.'

Amelia sighed. Little did Mrs Maggs know what she had done for her that day, or brought her to now!

Her good sense prevailed and she relaxed. Looking up, she answered the man across the table in a matter-of-fact voice: 'You're right. I couldn't go back to my old life at the Manor House and I would like to be able to work with you on the final stages of the book. But there's no reason why I shouldn't come to the Foundation on the same terms, as your assistant, is there? I could find a room in a small hotel or a hostel.'

'I want you to come as my wife,' he reiterated firmly.

'*Why?*' she asked, and the ache of her love for him

13

trembled a little in the insistence of her tone. But the flickering hope of hearing him say what she longed to hear was stillborn.

He shifted uneasily. 'I know it's a great deal to ask, but I want you beside me to share my home and my interests and my friends. I have a large, comfortable flat and a wide circle of colleagues. I'm sure you'll like them and fit in perfectly.'

Very flattering! she thought with wry resignation, and asked quietly: 'A sort of companion as well as assistant, to run the flat and help in any way I can? Is that what you mean?'

'No, damn it, that's not what I mean!' He rose from the chair and paced the room. Turning abruptly, he said: 'I mean a wife in the fullest sense,' his grey gaze held her upward glance with clear, forceful candour, 'and perhaps a child too, Amelia.'

Before she had time to interrupt him, he went on, 'I'm thirty-seven. In about two years I'm going back to my researches in Sarava. Anything could happen. I have—reasons for needing the assurance of an established family to leave behind me.'

All the tenseness, and the slight air of embarrassment which had showed occasionally, had evaporated and his manner was brisk and impersonal. 'Apart from my work I have a fairly substantial private income. I have only one living relative. I've been absorbed in my expeditions, my research and my books. Any thoughts of marriage I've had so far were in direct conflict with that and would have tied me down, but with you it's different. I want a wife and an heir, Amelia, and I'm offering you complete security for your future in return for the next two years of your life.'

There was profound silence between them. He was waiting, his face attentive but devoid of any sentiment. Amelia had to push words past the constriction in her throat.

'This is the strangest conversation I've ever had in my life,' she said helplessly, playing for time to take in the implications of his blunt statement.

'There isn't anyone else, is there?' he demanded. 'I've always had the impression——'

'No,' she cut in flatly. 'As we're being frank, I must tell you that I'm twenty-five and I have no emotional ties. There was a time, with someone at college, when I thought I might——' she broke off and looked down, concentrating on her hands clasped in her lap. 'I've never had any of the social graces I'm sure I would need as the wife of an important man like you. And as for—for giving you an heir, how could I possibly be sure of fulfilling my part of the bargain?'

'I'll take that chance, if you will.'

'Then it's a sort of bargain, isn't it,' she told him quietly, ruthlessly turning the knife in her own wounded feelings. 'Trying to make a go of it, on both sides. Just now you said that thinking about marriage had been different this time—with me. May I ask why?'

'Because you're intelligent and competent. Because you don't fuss over trivialities or chatter inanely. You have a sense of duty and compassion—I know how much you willingly gave up for your father, and I'm

15

sure you would give as much to any child of yours. What more can I say?' He settled down into his chair, stretched out his long legs, leaned back and clasped his hands behind his head. 'Frankly, Amelia, it's a relief to have found someone who doesn't indulge in romantic fantasies and who won't make emotional demands I can't meet. Time's too short, and I have enough problems on my hands before I go off to Sarava again. I trust you, and with me that means everything.'

Emma had decided that he was a cold fish—and he was. Amelia shivered involuntarily and remarked with a touch of astringency, before thinking, 'I wish Emma could hear this.'

He frowned suddenly. 'Do you propose discussing our concerns with your sister and brother-in-law? A prime bit of gossip for the village!'

'Good heavens, no!' she returned hastily, and his brow cleared.

'No, you're too self-possessed and mature to go rushing to Emma to pour out girlish confidences. Emma is delightful to look at, sociable and agreeable, perfectly adapted to her own sophisticated and aimless little world, but she talks too much. You're so unlike her, it's hard to remember you are sisters. You're much more——'

'Inarticulate?' she murmured dryly.

'I was going to say reticent,' the smile glinted in Lyne's eyes again. 'Even after a year of working closely together there are times when I haven't the slightest clue to your thoughts.' The grey glance caught and held hers deliberately for a second. 'At this moment I have no idea what's going on in those depths.'

'There are no depths,' she countered, looking away to protect her feelings at all costs.

'Oh, yes, there are. But I respect your right to keep them to yourself.' He picked up the cigarette packet, found it empty and tossed it with some force into the waste-paper bin.

'Well, that's about it. I can offer you escape and independence from the pressures of Emma's ethos, in exchange for a kind of partnership with me. I give you my word my claims on you will not be too tiresome and inconsiderate,' he saw the colour rise from her throat to her face and plunged on, 'and once I go back to Sarava you will be free, to all intents and purposes. I know you'll be discreet and sensible. A child, if we have one, will be a tie, of course, but one you would welcome, am I right?'

'I've always wanted to have children of my own,' she conceded in a low tone, chilled by the implication that he would never be returning from Sarava.

'Good. I'm glad we understand each other.'

He rose again and went to the window, expelling a brief sigh as if a weight had slipped from his mind. 'Compatibility, common interests and mutual respect, Amelia. That's a much sounder basis for living together than a brainstorm of physical attraction which fizzles out in rows and bitterness.'

The irony of it was cruel enough to snatch at her breath. There he was, so coolly, academically reasonable while that same physical attraction he despised so much was exerting such a strong pull on her that she was too bemused to reply. Her gaze clung to the lean tall back, the long square-tipped, capable hands, the thick hair shaping close to his head and into his neck. She ached to go to him, to have the right to touch him, to feel his arms hard around her binding her to him. The moment spun out. The longing built up until it was almost unbearable.

He turned his head and she dropped her glance, willing herself to breathe quietly and evenly.

'You'll want time to consider it,' he said, as though he had to set this against his own plans and schedules. 'I'm taking another month here before returning to town. If you agree to come with me, there are various arrangements to be made, including our marriage.' He paused. 'I don't want to rush you, but I like to be well organised—years of training for expeditions,' his mouth quirked humorously. 'This is Friday. Would it be asking too much to have your decision by, say, Monday?'

'That should be all right,' she replied sedately. 'I'll let you know.'

As if they had been discussing a house removal, or one of his minor forays into a jungle, thought Amelia, instead of one of the most significant decisions of her life! With quiet deliberation she picked up a new pencil and went back to checking through the page of typescript she had been working on before his proposal had shaken her out of her habitual appearance of imperturbability.

He stood looking at her down-bent head, the soft waves of brown hair drawn back and loosely rolled and pinned at the nape of her neck, the abstract air

18

of concentration and the unconscious little gesture of pushing her spectacles back on to the bridge of her nose. Unable to get her to look at him again, he thrust his hands into his pockets and moved away to the hall door.

'I think I'll take a walk down to the village, I need some cigarettes. You have a lot to mull over. Take the rest of the afternoon off.'

'Thank you,' she said. 'I'll just clear things away before I go.'

CHAPTER TWO

EMMA was lounging in a deep wing chair having tea when Amelia walked into the sitting-room of their private suite at the Manor. Her cup came down with a startled rattle on to the saucer.

'Good heavens, what are you doing back here at this time of day? Has the professor fired you or something?' She set the cup down on the silver tea service on the table beside her.

Amelia almost blurted out that, on the contrary, he had asked her to marry him. But she shut her teeth tight on the impulse, smiled a perfunctory smile and answered calmly: 'We decided to give it a rest for the weekend.'

'*We?*' Emma laughed exasperatedly. 'Oh, Melly, for goodness' sake don't get yourself so wrapped up in that peculiar man and his work. One of these days he'll be up and off to some godforsaken jungle and you'll be left sitting around here again! Honestly, you're beginning to identify yourself too much with him.'

'Is there enough in the pot? I didn't wait for tea at the cottage.'

'You haven't heard a word I've said, I might as well be talking to myself as usual.' Emma poured a cup of tea as Amelia laid her windcheater and scarf on the back of a chair. 'Ask Haskins to bring in another cup, Edward will be here in a minute.'

Amelia went out to the pantry and fetched the cup, knowing that the butler would be busy in the lounge of the club. On her return she picked up her own cup and sank into a chair.

Emma immediately started again on the subject, as though the opportunity to confront Amelia with the hard facts of her situation was not to be missed. 'Melly, do you know how much longer Professor Lyne is going to be here? Edward says he only leased the cottage for a year and as far as we know he hasn't renewed it. We're worried about you. This girl we've got now to look after the twins has settled in nicely and there's no question of getting rid of her for you to take over again, that's definite.'

'Mm-m,' Amelia responded absently, sipping her tea.

'Look, you must think about the future,' Emma rounded on her irritably. 'Pull yourself together! You're too complaisant. I don't know how you'll fend for yourself when this book thing comes to an end, as it soon will. There must be other jobs around like it. You ought to be making inquiries. Ask this man exactly how long he's going to need you, don't wait until it's all on top of you. He knows people at the Fenn Foundation, he could recommend you to his friends ...'

Her voice went on and on, sharp, bracing and impatient as she tried to penetrate her sister's preoccupied mood. Amelia looked around the sitting-room reflectively, as though she were seeing it for the first time. The sun streamed in through the tall french

21

windows which led to a terrace and a sweep of shorn grass as smooth as a bowling green. Long claret-coloured velvet drapes hung almost from the high, moulded ceiling to the polished parquet surround of the Persian carpet. The settee and chairs were solid and chunky, upholstered in glossy beige buttoned leather. The walls were hung with sporting prints, and there was a squat bookcase of sporting books and journals. A large colour television set occupied pride of place in the corner beyond the plaster columns of the fireplace, and the whole room was devoid of any personal touches. Even the vase of yellow and wine-red tulips, set on a pedestal stand between the velvet curtains, had a rigid formality like a wired display in a florist's window.

Amelia sighed, wondering what had prompted her to come here instead of quietly making herself a cup of tea in the pantry and taking it straight up to her own room. The unconscious need for company, she supposed. Emma was her sister, after all, the only one left of her family. If circumstances—and Emma—had been different, she would have been able to confide in her and talk out the nagging conflict of indecision that was going round in circles in her brain. But she felt completely alienated from the woman lounging in the chair opposite.

Emma was looking particularly beautiful in a turquoise jersey suit which enhanced the brightness of her blue eyes and her pale, smooth, delicately made-up skin. Her cap of shining gold hair was well sprayed, without a strand out of place. She had become a stranger; an elegant stranger waiting for the influx of weekend guests at the club.

The sense of Emma's antipathy was growing every minute, and if the Professor had done nothing else he had jolted Amelia out of her inertia into a realisation of just how strong it had become.

'... If you're afraid to tackle Professor Lyne yourself, Melly,' Emma was saying, 'there's no alternative but for me to ask Edward to broach it to him for you.'

'You'll do no such thing!' Amelia jerked her head round and faced her, a sudden flare of determination in her eyes. She had spoken quietly, and yet so positively that Emma's brows arched in astonishment.

'Well, really! There's no need to take umbrage!' she said shortly. 'We're only trying to help, you know! Do it yourself, if you prefer, but I should like to hear what your plans are before the summer season starts.'

Amelia laid her head back against the bulging squabs of the chair and regarded her sister.

'Emma, I'm grateful to you and Edward for finding room for me when Father died. But in all fairness, I've paid my own way—first with the little bit of money he left me and helping in any way I could, and more recently out of the generous salary Professor Lyne gives me. I don't live in a daydream, as you fondly imagine, we just function on different levels. All I can say is I'm sorry you've found my presence such an embarrassment.'

'Now that's foolish!' Emma protested, and had the grace to look uncomfortable. 'After the way you nursed and took care of Daddy we had to give you a break for a while, but Edward and I both feel that it isn't much of a life for you here, and it will be worse when the Professor goes.'

'Ah! You've been putting up with me for *Daddy's* sake,' murmured Amelia in a mocking tone. 'Well, you can safely assume you've done your duty now.'

'What do you mean?' Emma stared at her, taken aback by the palpable change in her sister's attitude. She had never known her to be caustic.

At this point Edward entered the room, a burly man immaculately turned out in jodhpurs and a hacking jacket, his boots gleaming, his hair slicked well back and his moustache trimmed close to his broad, handsome face.

'Amelia! You here? You feeling all right, old girl?'

'Perfectly, thank you, Edward.' Amelia turned and bestowed a glowing smile on him, the first genuine smile he had ever seen from her, which somehow transformed what he had always considered a plain face.

Disconcerted, he cleared his throat and smoothed his hair, glancing at his wife and saying, 'Fine, fine. Glad you could be home for tea.'

Amelia rose and put her cup on the tea tray. Standing beside Emma's chair, she looked down at her and said coolly: 'Don't worry, Emma. I can promise you, unreservedly, that I won't be an encumbrance much longer.' She picked up her windcheater and scarf. 'If you'll excuse me, I must go up to my room.'

As she was closing the door she heard Edward's gruff inquiry, 'What was all that about?' and Emma's,

'Don't ask me, I never know what's going on in her head ...' accompanied by an irritable clatter of the teapot on the tray.

Amelia crossed the hall quickly and went upstairs, and the sound of their voices faded behind her.

It wasn't difficult to avoid them for the rest of the weekend because the weather continued fine and the club was crowded with members and guests. On Saturday morning Amelia took the mid-morning bus to Whimpleford, the nearest market town. She changed her books at the library, did some shopping at Boots and Woolworths, and collected a pair of shoes from the menders. Later she treated herself to lunch in a small restaurant off Market Square and was lucky enough to get a small table to herself in a corner where, after a delicious chicken fricassée, fruit pie and cream and a glass of white wine, she sat sipping her coffee and musing sadly on the fact that she would not be frequenting this friendly little place much longer.

If there was one point she had now definitely resolved, it was that she would be leaving Whimpleford when Professor Lyne left, either as his wife, or independently to find a job elsewhere. He was not emotionally involved and would not hold it against her if she declined his offer of marriage, and she felt certain she could rely on him to help her get away from the Manor House. At the very least he would be able to provide her with the necessary references when she looked for a suitable place in London.

Amelia found herself wishing he could have been here with her, sharing her table in the quiet little restaurant, talking it over. How strange that they had never been out together! The professor had gone up to town occasionally to keep in touch with his department, but he had never invited her along and it had not occurred to her that he might ask her out.

All the more reason to be wary of his totally unexpected proposal of marriage, she thought, and her mind still shied away from committing herself. The notion went too deep with her and was too intimate for making a snap decision. She had not come to terms with it yet, and she resolutely put it aside for the time being.

Back in her own room, she looked at herself in the mirror. Once her reflection had shown a shapely figure, but living through so many anxious months had seemed to make her shrink. In the past year she had regained some weight, but the old dark green tweed suit and biscuit-coloured sweater still gave an impression of shabby make-do, and the colours made her skin look sallow.

The round hornrims cut across the thin planes of her oval face; she slipped her glasses off, leaning forward and peering a little. Suddenly she realised how vulnerable her moss-brown eyes looked without them, and she quickly replaced the frames. Her vision focused again, and so did her mind. At once she became calmer and able to cope.

Sunday passed much as usual, with Emma and Edward immersed in the club's activities. In the afternoon Amelia washed her hair and sat down to dry it in the old rocking chair which had once belonged to her grandmother and had been salvaged, in the teeth of Emma's derisive objections, from their old home. Rocking slowly to the rhythmic strokes of the hairbrush under the warm stream of the hand drier, Amelia faced the important problem that she must decide before the next morning.

Donovan Lyne had said that she had become indispensable to him. Here in the small village community it was probably true. Here he needed her, liked her, trusted her. But once he was back among his colleagues in his own academic world, what then? He had spent so much time studying human customs and foibles all over the world that even his own most personal relationships were subjected to the same cool, dispassionate appraisal. His admission that he had chosen her because she would not make any emotional demands on him had dismayed her with its chilling honesty. Such a bleak, expedient partnership—for reasons of his own. What reasons? Women? Clever, charming, sophisticated women who kept him from his work?

Her heart urged her to accept—with the hope that in two precious years with him she could try and change all that. Her head said no; his chief motive had been to settle his affairs conveniently, and their arid 'bargain' could become a kind of bondage from which she would never be free, specially if she had a child of his to remind her constantly that she had loved and lost him. And if she failed to give him the child which had seemed to be one of his main reasons for wanting to marry, the sense of her inadequacies would be even harder to bear than it was now.

She switched off the drier and sat very still, her

27

eyes closed, overwhelmed by the desire to accept and give herself to him completely, whatever the strains and stresses of their short time together. She tried to imagine what it would be like. He had never so much as attempted to touch her yet—except for the firm handclasp when he had first introduced himself there had been no physical contact between them at all. What kind of joy would she have in lovemaking that was a brief sexual transaction any woman would give him? For some women it might suffice. But Amelia's deepest nature required much more than that.

It was a long time before she rose from the chair and went to the mirror to comb out her hair. The swathe of soft brown tendrils hung down to below her shoulders, and as the comb ran through it natural waves sprang into place around her head. She coiled her hair haphazardly at the nape of her neck, pushing the pins in with trembling fingers, and wandered out to the tiny bathroom along the corridor to have a bath before slipping into her one and only black formal dress for the evening.

Amelia was a few minutes early the following morning, crossing the grounds of the estate and in through the hedge at the back of the apple trees. The professor must have been in the office waiting for her arrival, for she glimpsed him briefly at the window. Then he was coming across the grass to meet her.

She paused, standing under the flowering boughs. A year ago she had watched these trees blossoming and in a way she had begun to blossom again herself, emerging from the winter of loneliness in which she had been living. Now the tiny, tender apple buds were springing into rosy-white sprays along the bare branches once more, flecking the grass with drifting petals, and once more her life would change with the season.

Donovan Lyne was wearing a navy polo-necked sweater and cord slacks, the sleeves of the sweater pushed back up his tanned, sinewy forearms. The very sight of him after her restless, disquieting weekend turned Amelia's heart over. Casually she snapped off a low-hanging twig of blossoms, summoned a smile and called out, 'Good morning.'

He did not reply but came and stood before her, feet slightly apart, with his hands in his pockets. For a few seconds his grey eyes held hers with complete dominance. 'Well?' he asked abruptly, as if they had taken up their conversation without any need for preliminaries or equivocation.

'Professor, I ... I ...' she stopped, then resumed with considerable effort, 'I've thought it over very carefully, and I appreciate and thank you for paying me the biggest compliment of my life. But the answer is ... no.'

The rest of the week had the strangest quality of illusion. Amelia felt that she was living two separate lives; the quiet, dowdy, conscientious assistant working beside the professor with unruffled composure, and the lonely girl behind the façade, lost in a wasteland of regrets.

For one instant as she refused him she had imagined that his eyes had turned as bleakly grey as the North Sea, but it was so fleeting an impression that she supposed she must have been mistaken, for he had merely shrugged, saying with a short laugh: 'Don't look so conscience-stricken, Amelia. You aren't being constrained to marry for Emma's convenience—nor as a duty to me! So put your oversized conscience in cold storage, there's a good girl. I didn't ask you for reasons, whatever your decision. Let's forget it and get back to work.' And turning, he had strolled amiably beside her to the cottage.

Having arrived so painfully at the conclusion that she must reject his offer, Amelia was perversely feminine in secretly hoping he would try and change her mind—or at the very least look a little vexed—but his immediate acknowledgement of her refusal was cold comfort; ample proof that he had considered the matter quite objectively all along. He was probably prepared for a refusal and had other alternatives for settling his private affairs before he left England.

This was so wounding to her deepest feelings that it took her some days to settle down and give all her concentration to the book again. Her air of abstraction must have been more pronounced than usual, for she caught him watching her closely from time to time and she began to panic about her work, taking notes home and toiling late at nights to be able to keep a pace ahead of him. It would never do to have him think she was losing interest!

Yet the week went by without her finding the courage to ask him to take her with him when he left. It seemed a terrible imposition, bordering on impertinence in the circumstances. When she was thinking it out it had appeared so simple to enlist his advice and help. Now she no longer felt she had the right to expect anything of him.

It was not until the following week that he announced his intention of going up to town to the Fenn Foundation for a couple of days. He was in one of his restless moods, prowling about the office and frowning over a sheaf of typescript.

'Just a few pages which will need retyping while I'm away. After that it will be mainly clearing up before I leave here.'

Her heart plunged sickeningly. She must do something now ... *now*.

'Professor?' Glancing up, she encountered a long, narrowed look which made her hasten on a stronger note, 'When you return to the Institute I'm leaving Whimpleford too.'

His expression changed. The glint was back in his eye. 'Glad to hear it! From the agonised way you turned me down the other morning I assumed you'd opted for the quiet life at the Manor House again.'

She felt a spurt of anger at his flippant tone but said quietly, 'I told you I was finished with that.'

'It's a female's privilege to change her mind. However, I should have known you'd stick to your guns and get away from here.' He tossed the papers on his desk and added tersely, 'So it was just the notion of marrying me that proved distasteful—a salutary lesson for my ego!'

'Please, Professor ...' she began defensively, and he slumped in his chair and put his feet up on the desk and said: 'All right, Amelia, that chapter's closed. Made any plans about what you're going to do?'

'Not yet. I suppose I—I couldn't go on working with you?'

'You suppose right. You know the book's almost complete and will only need checking over. I phoned my department last week and they're already organised for my return to the fold.'

'Oh,' her hopes sank. 'Well, would you give me a reference? If I had something to show for this past year, with your name to back me up, I could start looking for a job as soon as I get to London.'

'I'll do better than that.' He paused reflectively, glanced at her anxious eyes and looked away. 'A friend of mine, Bill Austin, has been commissioned to do a series of monographs on the social structures of various primitive communities. He's up to his eyes in research and could do with an assistant. He and his wife, Polly, have a bungalow at Richmond, in the suburbs, and I'm sure Polly would enjoy having you staying with her.'

'That would be wonderful!' Her face lighted with pleasure, and the sweetness of her smile came as much of a surprise to him as it had to Edward. He sat up, staring at her in a bemused way as she said delightedly: 'I'm very grateful to you for suggesting it,' then hesitated. 'But I don't think I should plant myself on Mrs Austin like that. I'll find digs.'

'Get to know Polly first,' he advised. 'Once you've got the feel of the place and the job you can make your own arrangements.'

'I don't know how to thank you!'

'A chaste salute on the cheek, perhaps?' he recommended sardonically. It was so unlike him that the colour surged to her face, and he thumped his feet off the desk and rose. 'Don't look so affronted, Amelia, it was meant as a joke.' Taking out a cigarette, he flicked the lighter to it and blew a furl of smoke. 'You ought to meet and talk things over with Bill and Polly. What about coming up to town with me?'

'But the retyping on that chapter——'

'It can wait. We'll leave tomorrow morning and be back on Thursday evening. I'll phone and warn Polly so that she can put you up for the night.'

'Tomorrow?' said Amelia dubiously, her thoughts flying to her meagre wardrobe.

'I'll pick you up at the Manor House about eight. Will that suit?'

'Yes ... yes, of course. I was wondering about clothes.'

'I take it you mean something new?' he commented perceptively. 'Well, why not?'

'There won't be time now.'

'Hop on the afternoon bus to Whimpleford.'

'But all this work——'

'Can easily wait. I'd run you across myself, but my car's in the garage being checked over for the morning.'

The thought o fhis waiting around Whimpleford for her while she rushed about the shops looking for something suitable was not a welcome one anyway, and Amelia said earnestly: 'The bus will be fine. I always use the bus. Well, if you're sure you don't mind.'

CHAPTER THREE

AMELIA caught the bus with minutes to spare and reached Whimpleford on a cloud of unfamiliar euphoria.

In the department store in Market Square she bought a silky button-through dress in tawny brown with a demure turn-down collar of dark gold. It fitted her beautifully and had a classic simplicity of line; and to this she added the extravagance of a new wool velour stroller coat which was a remarkably good match.

She returned to the Manor House on the late bus, at a time she knew Emma and Edward would be in the club lounge, and went quietly up to her bedroom, hugging her purchases like a conspirator. There she spent a while ironing her black dinner dress, in case she needed it, polished up her old suitcase till it shone and packed a few changes of clothing.

At dinner she told Emma and Edward that she would be away for a couple of days, staying with friends of Professor Lyne's in London.

Emma stared at her for a moment and then started to laugh insinuatingly. 'Well, well! So you took my advice after all! I didn't anticipate his asking you up to town, Melly, but I'm glad you're making an effort.' Amelia winced inwardly, but smiled and changed the conversation, refusing to satisfy her sister's sharp-tongued curiosity.

Emma was still in bed the next morning when Amelia came downstairs, stroller coat over her arm and case in hand. Edward was crossing the hall and greeted her, looking rather startled at her appearance in the new dress with its long, slim-fitting lines.

'Very nice,' he said genially, 'smart as paint, old girl!'

Donovan Lyne's low-slung coupé swept round to the front steps. Amelia said: 'Goodbye, Edward, I'll be back tomorrow evening,' but he insisted on carrying her case out, and she hoped fervently that he wouldn't involve the professor in a lengthy conversation. However, they only exchanged the usual civilities about the weather as her case was stowed away. Edward held the door for her, the professor took the wheel beside her and the car moved swiftly down the drive of the Manor House.

Swinging out through the tall wrought iron gates, Amelia sat back and relaxed with a happy sigh, smiling faintly at the ludicrous thought that these were the portals of a very exclusive sort of jail from which she was escaping. She glanced unobtrusively at the man beside her. He looked different . . . his clothes, of course! The unmistakable cut of his car-coat in a supple dark brown suede, over an immaculately tailored charcoal-grey suit, the glimpse of a dark blue tie and pale blue collar, an edge of the same blue with gold cuff-links at his wrists. Professor Donovan Lyne, the distinguished anthropologist, not the man

36

at Appletree Cottage ... *the man who had asked her to marry him.*

No, not the same man at all. A formidable stranger who had wished her good-morning rather abstractedly and lapsed into silence. He was stern and impressive, and returning to his exclusive academic world. She had been right to refuse him, Amelia thought. With her gauche shyness and lack of chic she would never have fitted into his world, never in a month of Sundays, she thought wildly. All the joyful anticipation of the morning seeped out of her.

She took another quick glance. She might have been imagining it, but his profile looked unusually drawn. After she had left him perhaps he had had a call from someone who had upset him; or maybe he had worked till all hours of the night. Loving him as she did, and very sensitive to his moods, she was immediately filled with concern, but couldn't summon up the courage to ask if something was wrong.

As though he had read her thoughts he turned his head briefly and smiled. 'All set to face the world, Amelia? Leave your hang-ups behind with the typewriter and enjoy yourself. If that's the outfit from yesterday's shopping expedition, I like it.'

'Thank you.' She tightened her fingers on the handbag in her lap.

'By the way,' he added lightly, 'I couldn't get through to Polly on the phone. She must have taken the receiver off. She does that sometimes when she doesn't want Bill disturbed, and invariably forgets to put it back on the hook—to the exasperation of all concerned.'

'You mean ... she's not expecting me?'

'She's not expecting either of us,' he chuckled.

'Oh, but then I can't——'

'Forget it, Amelia. She'll be delighted, she loves surprises.' A pause. 'I wanted a word with Bill about the job for you too, but it's had to wait.'

Was this why he was out of sorts? Amelia felt troubled, not only at finding herself an uninvited guest to a stranger's house but because he sounded as if he were making a conscious effort at lightness.

'Look,' she offered tentatively, 'I can easily find a hotel room just for one night.'

'No, don't suggest that! Polly will be offended if you go off to a hotel instead of accepting her hospitality.'

And there the conversation ceased. Well, she thought, one of his professed reasons for liking her was that she didn't 'chatter inanely', so she kept quiet after that, deciding to wait until she had met Polly Austin before she insisted on finding a room elsewhere. The main thing was that she was with him, and she would let him take the initiative to converse or not as he chose.

Once they were on the motorway the coupé ate up the miles. About an hour later they passed a sign for an approaching service area and he broke the silence. 'Like a break for coffee?'

'If you like, but don't stop on my account. I had a good breakfast.'

'Well, if it's all right with you I'd rather push on,' he confessed. 'Polly will be sure to do the honours when we arrive.'

38

They left the motorway, entered the outer London suburbs near Richmond and at length turned into a tree-lined street which was obviously part of a private housing estate. The bungalow was on a corner and although the sky was overcast and it had begun to drizzle, the mellow red brick walls and red-tiled roof had a welcoming aspect. A crooked old lilac tree drooped from the trim hedge and a long trellis of rambler roses on the south wall was thick with glossy new leaves.

The professor came round and opened the door for Amelia, turning up his coat collar against the rain. In his town clothes he appeared to be even taller and leaner—and for a second or two she felt a jaded tenseness in him as if he was forcing himself to make a great effort.

'Make a run for it and ring the bell. I'll get your case.'

Amelia hurried across the pavement and up the flagged path to the front door. She heard the chimes ringing, and pressed into the tiny porch out of the wet. There were muffled voices and footsteps, and the door opened on a plump middle-aged woman in slacks and a hand-knitted yellow sweater, her ample form bulging comfortably over the ties of a flowered apron. Her lips rounded 'Oh!' in surprise and her hands flurried round behind her to untie and whisk off the apron.

'Sorry!' Her hazel eyes sparkled cheerfully at Amelia. 'I was hoping you were the milkman. No, I don't mean that, of course ... oh, dear! ... do come in. Do you want to see Bill——?' and then, with her whole face lighting up and laughing: 'Don! You wretch, I wasn't expecting you today! What are you doing here? Come in, come in, you'll get soaked.'

Amelia backed into the hall, out of the way, as Polly fell into the professor's arms, lifting her face and pulling his head down to kiss him. A short, stout, balding man with rimless spectacles came into the hall and as he pumped the professor's hand vigorously Mrs Austin turned and clasped Amelia's arms, squeezing them gently and saying with undeniable delight, 'You must be Amelia Leigh! Of course you are! Don's told us all about you. I've been nagging him for months to bring you to see us. How long can you stay, Amelia? Bill, this is Don's Amelia.'

Don's Amelia ... the words echoed round in her head as Bill Austin shook her hand in a crushing grip, and her eyes went involuntarily to the professor's to find them glinting with the friendly amusement and warmth they had shared the previous afternoon. Her spirits began to rise again, and her awkwardness and restraint dissolved as they shed their coats and were ushered into a long, comfortable sitting-room overlooking the side garden.

Amelia almost disappeared into the downy depths of a large old-fashioned chair covered in a soft cream coloured slip-cover like the rest of the suite. Jade green wall-to-wall carpeting and a scatter of bright cushions gave the room a light, airy appearance in spite of the clutter of books and magazines, bundles of knitting wool, little tables, china ornaments, vases of flowers and potted plants.

Polly was still overwhelming Professor Lyne with

40

a stream of affectionate inquiries and reproaches. He put one arm round her plump waist and his hand over her mouth, giving her a little shake.

'You took the phone off the hook yesterday—right?'

She drew his hand away, looking up at him in comic dismay. 'Oh, good heavens! Yes! Bill's been up to his eyes in it, and it's the only way to stop the beastly jangle. Are you staying in town or going back today?'

'We planned to stay overnight and drive back to Whimpleford tomorrow evening.' He flung himself into a chair and stretched out his long legs.

'Meetings at the Foundation?' Bill Austin asked him.

'One this afternoon and one tomorrow morning. Will you put Amelia up for the night?'

'Of course,' Polly beamed, 'and you too. It won't be the first time you've slept on the couch.'

'Not me, Polly, my pet. I'll go over to my flat. It needs looking over anyway before I move in again in a few weeks.'

'Oh, Don!' she wailed. 'Why didn't you let me know? Nobody's been near the place for about three months, it'll be dusty and unaired and cold and cheerless. Must you go there?'

'I've been getting soft in the country after years in the jungle, one spartan night under my own cheerless roof will do me good,' he grinned. 'I want to open it up and see what needs to be done, arrange to have it thoroughly spring-cleaned, get the telephone recon-

nected and have some of my books and papers un-
crated.'

'Marguerite and I planned to give it a real going
over pretty soon so that it would be all spick and
span when you arrived,' sighed Polly. 'Ah, well, I
know it's no use trying to budge you, you stubborn
creature.'

'Polly, you're an angel, but I can't let you and
Marguerite wear yourselves out doing a thankless job
like that for me.'

Amelia, who had been watching the professor in
silence, noticed lines about his mouth and eyes and a
thin crease between his brows. Who was Marguerite?
It suddenly struck her how little she knew of his
friends and his personal life, how little he had talked
of them. All she knew of his background came from
newspaper reports and a magazine article she had
once read.

Polly was saying: 'All right, but you must have
proper meals, Don. Promise me? Oh, how thought-
less of me, you're both dying for some coffee, I'm
sure!'

Amelia rose at once. 'May I help?'

'Would you, dear?' Polly led the way, picking up
Amelia's case and taking it to a small guest room
along the hall from the sitting-room. It was simply
furnished in blue and white, with checked folk-weave
at the window and a flounce of blue candlewick on
the bed. 'Like to freshen up? The bathroom's opposite.'

'Mrs Austin, it's very kind of you——'

'Nothing of the sort!—and do please call me

Polly, Amelia.' She patted Amelia's arm and whisked off to the kitchen at the end of the hall.

When Amelia joined her in the kitchen there was a delicious aroma of coffee from a large, earthenware pot by the stove.

'I love having people to stay,' Polly said, putting a tray on the kitchen table. 'I've been dying to meet you, Amelia, Don's been singing your praises for months. I was eaten up with curiosity, but we had strict orders to keep away from the cottage so that he could relax and get on with his work and not have to bother with entertaining. Cups in the cupboard over there, dear.' She put on a pan of milk to warm as Amelia opened the cupboard. 'How on earth do you manage Don? You'll have a job seeing he doesn't overdo things once he's back in town. Meetings, lectures, social engagements, and work, work, work. Marguerite and I could never get him to let up in the old days, and after five years he's become more autocratic and impossible than ever! But I expect you know how to go about it better than we ever could. I suppose you'll be going with him to look the flat over?'

'No,' Amelia said quietly, keeping her eyes down as she set the cups.

'No?' Polly tilted her grey head as though surprised. 'But I thought, from what Don said——' she broke off, flicked a shrewd glance at Amelia's calm, expressionless face and turned away to remove the milk from the stove. Her back was to Amelia as she stooped and brought out a large pottery crock of biscuits. Amelia longed to ask her what it was the pro-

43

fessor had said, because her kindly, open manner was the sort that invited confidences, but an instinctive reserve held the words back.

Polly took out a biscuit and munched it as she put the crock on the table. 'I shouldn't eat these because it results in this!' she announced cheerfully, indicating her ample hips. 'But I can't resist them. No will power, Bill says.' Then gently, on a serious note: 'Aren't you coming up to London when he comes, Amelia?'

'Yes, if I can find a suitable job.' Amelia poked her spectacles up the bridge of her nose in the tell-tale gesture the professor would have recognised, and explained, rather hesitantly, that she had been hoping there might be a possibility of her working with Polly's husband.

'With Bill? Oh, Amelia, I'm so sorry! But I think —no, I'm sure, Bill has a girl starting on Monday, one of his old students.'

'Has he? Well, never mind.' Amelia smiled at her rueful face, fighting down the desperate sense of disappointment that swept over her. 'Perhaps something else will turn up one of these days.'

'Well, of course!' Polly rushed in reassuringly. 'Between them, Bill and Don know all the right people and they'll soon fix you up with something that suits you.' She still looked faintly puzzled, as if there were one or two pertinent questions she would have liked to ask, but all she said was: 'You must come and stay with us, for as long as you want, Amelia. We'd love to have you here. The room's just crying out to be used! You take the biscuit crock while I bring the tray in. Lead the way and we'll tackle the two of them about it over coffee.'

The men rose as they entered, Bill taking the tray from his wife and putting it on the table in front of her chair. She poured, and as Bill passed the cups and offered biscuits, she said thoughtfully: 'You look tired, Don. Are you rushing things to get back to London?'

'Not really, but I have a fairly busy schedule lined up now.' He changed the subject by complimenting her on the coffee. 'Mrs Maggs could do with a few lessons from you about making it, Polly.'

Polly exchanged a quick glance with her husband, which was not lost on Amelia, and plunged immediately into the subject of the possibilities of a job for Amelia in town, demanding that Bill support the invitation to her to make a home with them for as long as she wished. Bill Austin backed up the offer unreservedly. It was apparent that he and Donovan had been discussing the job prospects too.

What a nice couple these Austins were! thought Amelia, studiously avoiding the professor's eye as the two men bandied names and likely openings among the various educational projects financed by the Fenn Foundation. She could understand that Donovan might feel some sense of obligation to help her, but Bill Austin also seemed genuinely concerned, like an old friend. She sat quietly, listening and answering a few questions. All the while she was realising how much she had missed in the last few years in not having the kind of personal friends to help and advise her in the direction of her own talents and interests.

45

Some while later Donovan flicked back his cuff to look at his watch and rose with a visible effort quite unlike his usual nervy strength.

Polly protested: 'Won't you at least stay for lunch, Don?'

'No can do, Polly, but thanks. I have to be at a meeting of the Fenn Council at two-thirty. Will you all have dinner with me tonight? I thought the Chancery Hotel—it's quiet and civilised, and the food is excellent.'

'Sorry, old man, but Polly and I have a dinner date with the Andersons, fixed up last week,' replied Bill. 'You two go out and enjoy the bright lights.'

'Amelia?' said the professor. 'Will you join me?'

'Thank you, I'd like that,' she accepted rather shyly, concealing her eagerness for another precious hour or two in his company as some consolation for her bitter disappointment about the job.

'I'll call back for you here, say at about seven?'

Amelia made a tentative offer to meet him in town, but he wouldn't hear of it. His eyes rested on her for a long moment as he shrugged into his coat, then he kissed Polly, shook hands with Bill, said, 'I'll see you later, Amelia,' and was gone.

As she heard the car pulling away from the kerb, Amelia was conscious of a terrible void. After a year of working so closely with him, knowing he would be in the little cottage on the far side of the Manor House estate as a reassuring certainty whenever things became difficult with Emma and Edward, it came home to her for the first time, with stunning force, just how bleak her future was going to be. How was she going to face up to the reality of severing the close tie of day-to-day contact? She would have to learn to live with this parting permanently, until time had mercifully filled it with other interests and healed it. Even if she had agreed to marry him she would have had to steel herself to the inevitable—that he would return to Sarava.

She told herself it would not have worked out anyway. She had realised that this morning. Nevertheless the thought that she had refused to share the two years he had offered her, two whole years together, swept over her in a dark tide of remorse.

CHAPTER FOUR

POLLY Austin exchanged another of those wordless signals of understanding with her husband, who promptly retired to work in his study as she led Amelia back into the sitting room.

'Sure you wouldn't like another cup of coffee?' As Amelia shook her head, murmuring thanks, Polly picked up a bundle of multi-coloured knitting. With her head bent over the busy click of needles she asked: 'Amelia, why don't you—stay on with Don?'

'The book's virtually finished, and his department can provide all the assistance he needs once he's back there,' returned Amelia.

'Ah!' Polly stopped for a second, ostensibly counting stitches. 'I hope he's going to settle down now. He's always been so restless, living on a tightrope of nervous energy, yet so self-sufficient one can't get near enough to really help him. Did you know he's been offered the top post as Director of the Fenn Institute of Anthropology? Oh, dear, I shouldn't have mentioned that! It isn't official yet. But we're all anxious to know if he'll accept. We think he should, not only for his own sake, the Institute needs someone dynamic to take over. Bill and I began to think that you might be the one to influence him to stay.'

'*Me*?' Amelia smoothed her skirt over her knees, and managed to continue in a commendably steady voice. 'No, Polly, he hasn't even spoken about the Directorship to me. As far as I know he's planning to go back to Sarava in a couple of years.'

'*What*? Oh no!' Polly exploded in exasperation. 'He's obsessed with that disease-infested place, killing himself over those wretched bloodthirsty tribes! It's lunacy to waste a brilliant mind like his shut away on a volcanic island with nothing but jungle and heat for the rest of his life. He must have studied every single trivial detail about them while he was there. How much more does he need? You've worked on his book, so you know.' She cast her knitting aside in disgust. 'Oh, Amelia!'

With a mounting sense of dismay, Amelia wavered. 'It's ... it's his decision.' If he had been offered such an important post at the Institute, why was he determined to go back to Sarava? she wondered miserably.

Polly apologised ruefully. 'I'm sorry for that silly outburst, but I'm as fond of him as if he were my own brother. When he was a youngster we were neighbours and he practically lived in our home. Bill was a close friend too—that's how I met my husband. Bill and I have been so happy, we've been longing to see Don married to a woman who would give him the same happiness and the incentive to stay put.'

Amelia leaned her head back against the chair, her face turned away from the window light to shield her expression. She was pale and silent.

'Years ago,' sighed Polly, 'we thought he might marry Marguerite, Bill's youngest sister. They were inseparable and he seemed crazy about her. But it must have been one of those passing phases because as soon as he was offered the chance of taking over the Saravan expedition he jumped at it. Poor Marguerite! She's rather delicate, and loves her creature comforts. If she'd been stronger and really loved him she'd have tied him down then, or gone with him. I think it was just an immature infatuation. About a year later she married Tom Anderson, and as for Don—well, he's changed a lot since he returned from the East Indies.'

She paused, taking surreptitious peeps at Amelia to see if her colour was improving, and then went on talking in a casually reflective tone.

'He was so ill out there—that may account for some of it, I suppose, but he doesn't discuss things or confide in us as he used to. The few times he's come to London, or we've talked on the phone, he's always spoken of you, Amelia. How thoughtful and practical you are, how lucky he was to find you in Whimpleford, how marvellously you two get on together. Bill and I were beginning to hope that you ... that you and Don ...' her voice dropped lamely.

She seemed to be waiting and Amelia said, 'It wouldn't work out, Polly.'

'Wouldn't it?' Polly gave up the pretence of knitting, looked at Amelia's clenched hands and up to meet her eyes. Amelia looked away.

Polly bundled her knitting up and pushed it into a bag. 'Forgive me, dear, don't be upset. I didn't mean to pry in a gossipy way. Bill says I'm a romantic old busybody, but I want my friends to be happy, that's all I care about.' She sighed again, shaking her head, and began collecting the cups on to the tray. Amelia got up to help, aching to unburden herself of the whole story but still too withdrawn and cautious.

In the kitchen as Polly rinsed and she dried, Polly said: 'You will come and stay with us, Amelia? Do say yes.'

'I'd like to very much, but don't you think it would be more sensible to wait until I have one or two jobs in view before I move to town?'

'Far better if you're here on the spot. Once you've cleared things up for Don in Whimpleford you'll be free, won't you? Nothing to hold you there? Well then!' With blithe, almost childlike transparency she went on, 'The present Director of the Institute won't be retiring until the end of the year, so there'll be plenty of time to bring Don to his senses—in more ways than one! He's sure to visit us quite a bit, you know.'

It was clear she had guessed Amelia's feeling for Donovan and was determined to take a hand. Amelia, heartsore and despondent a few minutes before, began to laugh helplessly. Polly eyed her in surprise, then started laughing too.

'I *am* a busybody!' she conceded, relishing it with a twinkle. 'So be warned, Amelia! I'll nag you all day today and tomorrow until you agree to come to us.'

Amelia suddenly felt as if she had known Polly Austin for years, and far from resenting this intrusion into her private life was warmed and cheered by it. She also had a wonderful evening to look forward to.

After a light lunch of a delicious cheese soufflé and fresh fruit, the two of them went to Richmond in

51

Polly's scarlet Mini and did the household shopping. Then they went to the top of the hill to look down on the winding curve of the Thames in the little valley, and took a slow drive through Richmond Park before returning home.

Bill had joined them in the sitting room for tea when the phone rang, and he answered it in his study. They heard the distant murmur of his voice, and Polly said, 'Wonder who that could be?'

Bill came to the door. 'Amelia? Don would like a word with you.'

She followed him to the book-lined room and picked up the receiver.

'Amelia?'

'Yes, Professor.' She answered tonelessly; somehow she knew what was coming and shrank back from it, leaning heavily against Bill's desk.

'We've just taken a break from the meeting. It looks like going on quite late ...' there was silence for a moment.

'Professor?' she faltered.

'Yes, I'm still here. I'm afraid it's off tonight, Amelia. There isn't much I can do about it.'

Through the constriction in her throat she said, 'That's all right. I understand.'

'I hope it won't spoil your evening entirely. There'll be other times—give me a rain check?'

'Of course. Please don't worry about me.'

'Bill's coming up to town tomorrow afternoon,' he told her. 'Bring your case with you. He'll drop you off at the Institute. Ask for me at the commissionaire's desk,' the abrupt, detached phrases beat against her ear. 'I'll show you round and introduce you to a few people. Then we can have something to eat and drive straight down to Whimpleford. Suit you?'

'Fine, if you're sure I won't be a nuisance.'

'You're never that. Entrance hall tomorrow then, three o'clock.'

There was something odd in his tone and she said quickly, 'I won't keep you now, Professor, you must be busy. I'll be there at three.'

'Busy ... yes ... sorry about this evening. See you tomorrow, Amelia. Till then——' the line clicked, cutting off his blurred voice.

Slowly she replaced the receiver. She shouldn't have come on this visit; she had known it since morning, felt in her bones that there was something amiss with him right from the start. She took off her spectacles and brushed her hand over her eyes. Replacing the thick frames carefully, she composed her face and returned to the other room.

Bill had evidently already told Polly what the call was about, for her plump cheeks were pink with vexation. 'What did I tell you, Amelia? Don and his work!'

'Amelia can come with us,' Bill insisted cordially. 'My sister Marguerite and her husband Tom Anderson,' he smiled at Amelia. 'It'll be an informal party, with a bit of bridge afterwards. You're more than welcome.'

To be confronted with Donovan's first love—perhaps his only love? She refused lightly and tactfully, making the excuse that she would like to go up to town anyway; she hadn't been to the West End for years and would love to see a show or a film. She was so animated and enthusiastic about it that they seemed convinced, and the rest of the time was spent in discussing possible shows, and what buses and trains she would take.

Amelia was used to solitude and did not mind getting away from the Austins on her own. Strolling down Regent Street, window-gazing in the soft early twilight, she made her way across Piccadilly Circus and went into a cinema in the Haymarket, but the film bored her. She left early and found a little coffee-bar where she had a snack and sat watching the London crowds through the plate glass window until she judged that Bill and Polly must have left home for their dinner date. Then she travelled back by train and bus and let herself quietly into the silent house with the latch-key they had given her.

She had a bath and retired to bed, but not to sleep. Her mind was on Donovan Lyne, as it had been all evening. Where had he been while she was wandering aimlessly around, killing time? Right there in the heart of town working ... or spending the evening with someone else? There were plenty of women, even if Marguerite was no longer available. A host of wounding conjectures crowded in on her in the small, dark, unfamiliar room, and it was not until after she heard the Austins come in that she eventually fell asleep.

Bill drove her to the Institute after lunch the next day, turning into a quiet square off Holborn and pulling up in front of an imposing grey stone building with a columned portico. He carried her case into the entrance hall, crushed her hand in a tight grip as he repeated the invitation to come and stay with them, and apologising for his haste, hurried off to keep his own appointment.

Amelia's footsteps echoed through the large hall as she crossed the parquet flooring to the inquiries counter. It was just on three o'clock.

'Can I help you, madam?'

'I'm Miss Leigh, Professor Lyne's assistant from Whimpleford. Would you please let him know I've arrived?'

The uniformed commissionaire looked taken aback: 'He hasn't been in today, not so far as I know.'

'Well,' she glanced diffidently down at her case, 'I have instructions to meet him here. May I wait? I expect he'll be here shortly.'

'Of course, madam. Please take a seat.'

She perched on the edge of a leather-covered seat opposite the counter, scanning the portraits of dignitaries in heavy gold frames along the walls, listening to voices reverberating on the stairs, watching the hands of the clock above the counter crawl slowly round. Occasionally the lifts whirred, the gates clashed. People passed in and out of the building and she encountered more than one curious glance.

When almost three-quarters of an hour had gone by all her diffidence had evaporated. Suppressing a mounting sense of annoyance at being kept hanging about like a recalcitrant student, without even the courtesy of a message explaining the professor's delay, she went back to the counter.

'It's quite unlike the professor to be so late for an appointment without leaving word. Perhaps there's a note. Please check.'

The man looked through the long range of pigeon-holes behind his desk and turned again, apologetically shaking his head. 'I'm sorry, Miss Leigh. Could there be some mistake about the day?'

'No,' she said firmly. 'We're returning to the country this evening.'

'Just one moment.' He dialled the wall phone behind him. 'There's a Miss Leigh here at the reception desk. Appointment with Professor Lyne ... yes, miss ... did he say? ... no, there's nothing left down here. Very well, miss, I'll tell her.' He looked at Amelia with some concern this time. 'They haven't heard from the professor today upstairs in his department either, madam. He was due at a meeting this morning, but he didn't come in.' He cleared his throat uncomfortably. 'The professor is his own master, as you might say. They thought he'd changed his mind and decided to go back to Whimpleford already.'

'But he wouldn't leave without——' she bit back the rest. The truth was that his behaviour, even his manner, had been strangely offhand since they had come up to London. Could it be that Donovan Lyne was subtly punishing her—the notion suddenly pierced her—punishing her for refusing him? But that was ridiculous!

He had simply forgotten her. Preoccupied as he was with his work, his colleagues and the forthcoming move to the flat, his arrangement to meet her had been swept aside by something else. Heaven alone

56

knew where he was, or when he would remember her—probably when he was driving back down the M4 with an empty seat beside him! she decided bitterly.

Her next thought was to ring Polly Austin, but she rejected it. She was not returning lamely to the Austins, crying for help. She would go back to Whimpleford by train, and take her humiliation with her.

As her temper rose so did her calm, icy dignity, and the commissionaire said anxiously, 'I would try and check with the Professor's flat, madam, but the phone isn't connected yet.'

Amelia cut him short by asking if he could tell her the train times from Paddington. He produced the rail guide, thumbed through it and gave her the details. She looked at the clock; it was well past four.

'In case the professor should come here after all, please tell him I'm catching the five-fifteen,' she said coolly. 'And I should like the professor's address so that I can leave a note there too, if I have time.'

'Certainly, madam.' He wrote it on a notepad, stripped it off and passed it to her. 'I'm sorry there's been this misunderstanding, madam.'

'That's all right. Thank you.' She collected her case, refused his offer to call her a taxi and walked out.

A few moments later she picked up a cab in Holborn and was on her way to Paddington Station. As they moved through the gathering traffic of the rush hour the spurt of anger which had buoyed her up slowly faded, to be replaced by the frightening sense of loss which had assailed her when Donovan had left the Austins' house the previous day. She should have waited, however late he was. Both her pride and her love had been badly bruised, but he was, above all, her employer and she owed it to him to make at least one more attempt to contact him. She would try his flat.

Knocking on the glass partition, she gave the cabby the address of the flat. 'Traffic's thickening up, miss,' he counselled, 'you might lose your train.'

'Never mind, I'll take a chance on that.'

At length the cab turned into a street in Kensington and pulled up. Three large Victorian houses had been converted into a luxury block, its white paint gleaming, its façade of tall bow-shaped windows decorated with the tracery of black wrought-iron balconettes. Amelia asked the cabby to wait and went in. The entrance was thickly carpeted, as was the curved staircase at the end. A small man in dark blue uniform, with his hair neatly plastered down, came out of the porter's booth.

'Do you know if Professor Lyne is here at his flat?' she asked.

'Yesterday he was, miss. Haven't seen him today.' He glanced out through the front door. 'His car's still parked along there. He must be.'

She recognised it herself then, and suddenly smiled at the porter. So he hadn't left for Whimpleford without her! 'Flat Two, isn't it?'

'First floor, front,' he agreed.

Restraining a desire to run up the staircase, Amelia took it sedately, her feet sinking into the carpeting.

The first landing was very quiet, with two short corridors on either side and right in front of her, opposite the stairs, a white door numbered '2' with a lion's head knocker and discreet bell-knob in polished brass.

With a slightly tremulous hand she pressed the door-bell and stepped back, pushing up her spectacles and straightening the collar of her coat as she waited. A minute went by in silence. Thinking that she might not have pressed it hard enough, she rang again much more firmly. Another minute, and still no reply. It occurred to her that although Donovan's car was parked outside he could have gone out with someone else. One more try—she lifted the knocker and rapped hard.

Accept the fact, she told herself forlornly, he isn't in. If she waited too long she would miss the train and the next one would get her to Whimpleford too late for the last bus to the village. It would be best to leave a message with the porter.

Turning away to the head of the stairs, she caught the sound of a dragging movement behind the door and a slump against the panels. She spun round, her heart in her mouth, and grasping the door knocker rattled it urgently.

'Professor? Is that you?' A premonition swept through her and into her alarmed voice. 'Professor, open the door! *Don, please* ...'

The door seemed to give way under the pressure of her hand, but slowly, laboriously, as the weight gradually shifted. Instinctively she pushed into the room.

59

Donovan Lyne teetered against the side wall. His face was drawn and grey, and rough with a stubble of beard. He was clad only in a pair of pyjamas and his body was shaking, and when she put her arms out to support him she felt the burning fever on his skin.

CHAPTER FIVE

AMELIA succeeded in getting him back to the bedroom by hitching his right arm across her shoulders and exerting all her strength to help him. The whole flat was still swathed in dust sheets; he had pulled the cover off the bed and had been sleeping on bare mattress and pillows with a couple of blankets. His case was open, considerably jumbled, his clothes were strewn on the floor.

She hastily thumped the pillows, heaved his legs on to the bed and pulled the blankets over his shivering form.

'Touch of fever ... that's all ...' he muttered vaguely.

'Yes—I know.' She tucked the blankets close around his shoulders and under his chin. 'What's the name of your doctor?' He shut his eyes and she put out a hand and turned his face, saying imperatively: 'Tell me the name of your doctor, Professor. *Your doctor.*'

'Hallow ... tropical medicine ...'

'Fine, now you can relax. Nothing more to worry about.'

She turned to the door, gripping the lintel for a second and pressing her knuckles against her trembling lips. Then she slipped off her coat, threw it across an unopened crate in the front room and called out for the porter from the top of the stairs. Although she appeared completely calm, something in her tone brought the little man running up the flight two at a time.

'The professor is ill, and I can't phone from the flat. Do you have a telephone?'

'Yes, miss, sure thing.'

'I must stay with him. Please look up the number of Dr Hallow, the specialist in tropical medicine, and ask him to come as soon as he can.'

The porter nodded. 'I know the doctor, miss— used to visit the prof regular.'

'That's a relief.' Amelia went back into the flat, leaving the door on the latch. Her mouth was dry. She found the kitchen off the narrow hall, beautifully appointed with matching units but bare, without any crockery, glassware or utensils in sight. On one of the stainless steel tops lay a packet of meat sandwiches and an empty waxed carton with coffee dregs—the stale, untouched sandwiches told their own story of how he must have been feeling since yesterday. Rinsing out the carton, she filled it at the cold tap and sipped it. At least the taps were functioning, but there was neither gas nor electricity to heat water if it was needed.

She refilled the carton and took it into the bedroom. Donovan was dozing, and gazing down into his stubbled, exhausted face she reproached herself for all her foolish speculations about him. That he might be ill had not occurred to her, for he was always so vital and self-assured. Had he had milder attacks of this at Whimpleford too? Those mornings when he had been unusually taciturn and gone off in his car for a break, as he called it, were more probably visits to the doctor in Whimpleford. Why had he never mentioned it to her? she wondered miserably. She felt so helpless and frightened. Pulling a dust cover off a chair, she sat beside him, silently watching him with her heart in her eyes.

A subdued rapping startled her to her feet and out to the door.

'O.K., miss. The doc's just got back to his consulting rooms. Says he'll be over in half an hour. Oh, miss!—the cabby's still waiting.'

Amelia gasped. 'I'd forgotten! Tell him I won't be going to Paddington, and ask him to bring in my case, please.'

Money for the cab—where had she left her handbag? She found it on the floor behind the door of the flat, and extracting her wallet she flicked through the notes. There were essentials she would need. As she hadn't spent any of the money she had brought with her, there seemed enough for the moment. Anxiously she had another look at Donovan Lyne and then went down to the entrance.

The cabby looked a bit surly as he stood waiting beside her case, but she was too preoccupied to notice his impatience. She paid the fare and was adding a generous tip when a thought struck her. 'Are there any shops near here?'

'High Street round the corner,' the porter supplied.

'If I give you a list, will you fetch me some things I need?' she appealed to the driver. 'It'll be quickest by cab before the shops shut.'

'Well . . .' he began reluctantly, but she had already started writing on the back of the slip of paper with the professor's address.

'She can't leave . . . he's taken bad and the doc's coming,' she heard the porter confiding, 'and I gotter stay put for the flats.'

'Here you are—just some milk, eggs and bread and a few other essentials.' Amelia handed the cabby the list and a sheaf of notes. 'Oh, and some candles and matches, and something to cook on. One of those cheap little camping stoves, I'm sure you'll know what to get.'

'No gas or electric turned on up there yet,' the porter explained.

'Want the number of my cab?' the other asked more cordially.

'No, why should I?' said Amelia.

'All this money,' he replied awkwardly.

'I trust you,' Amelia told him simply. 'In fact, I'm depending on you—both of you,' she included the porter, and turning away went back upstairs, unaware of the impression she had made on the two men with her gentle appeal for help.

There was nothing more she could do except bide her time, but she had to have something to occupy her hands and submerge her distress. Moving quietly around the bedroom, she removed all the dust covers and carefully folded them, picked up Donovan's clothing and tidied it away in the long fitted unit that lined one wall, and in doing so discovered an enclosed dressing top, on which she placed his toilet articles, and a series of drawers which served as a linen press.

Here she found bed-sheets and towels as well as extra blankets and a duvet, all clean, but unaired and smelling of mothballs.

The drawers moved smoothly and silently, and she realised that although the room was austere and masculine it had been expensively furnished. The carpet was dark grey, the venetian blinds pale grey, the chairs and bedhead upholstered in royal blue and white striped silk. It was such a contrast with the shabbiness of the cottage at Whimpleford, yet Amelia suddenly yearned to be back in its happy, thread-bare security.

Donovan Lyne groaned, moving restlessly and pushing the blankets off. She hurried to his side, on her knees beside the bed. His forehead was beaded with sweat now, and she had a struggle to keep the blankets round him. 'Don ... please, Don,' she coaxed distractedly, 'the doctor will be here soon.' She smoothed back his hair, willing him to stop fighting her and relax, and after a few minutes he became quieter under the cool, persuasive touch of her fingers. How often she had longed to run her fingers through his thick dark hair—but never like this. This was the other face of love, the urgent need to comfort and protect.

He suddenly opened his eyes, looked blankly at her and said: 'I must ring Amelia.'

'Yes, well,' she swallowed convulsively, 'it doesn't matter now.'

'Tell her ... can't get back tonight ...' he mumbled, fidgeting with the blankets again.

'I'll tell her,' Amelia responded firmly, and he

seemed to accept it, for she was able to raise his head in the crook of her arm and hold the carton to his lips. When he had drunk a little water he lay back and closed his eyes once more.

Amelia crouched beside his bed, holding the blankets down for what seemed like a lifetime until the door-bell rang. She scrambled up almost wearily, rubbing her eyes and shaking out her skirt, and composed herself for whatever the doctor's verdict might be.

She opened the door, still blinking a little at the brighter light of the landing. 'Dr Hallow?' She offered her hand to a thick-set man with a slight stoop. 'I'm Amelia Leigh. I'm glad you were free to call so quickly.'

'Ah, yes, Amelia Leigh.' He was bluff and assertive. 'I've heard of you, and you know Truscott, an old colleague of mine in Whimpleford who's been keeping an eye on Donovan Lyne.'

'I've met Dr Truscott,' she replied steadily. 'Please come in.' To the porter hovering in the background she said; 'I'll leave the door on the latch. When the cabby returns would you put everything into the kitchen for me?'

Dr Hallow strode into the bedroom with the assurance of an old friend who knew both the flat and its owner well. For some reason Amelia found herself making halting apologies for the condition of the place, which he brushed aside, asking her briskly to raise the venetian blinds to get the most of the late evening light.

She obeyed, then stood in silence at the window

66

and stared out with unseeing eyes as the doctor carried out his examination. She heard the click of the clasps on his medical case and tightened a clammy palm on the sash-cord to which she was clinging.

His brisk, robust voice made her jump. 'Well now, you're inordinately quiet, Miss Leigh,' and turning, she saw the doctor intent on preparing a hypodermic syringe. 'Like to fill me in on what's been happening?'

Amelia told him simply and concisely as much as she knew, and explained that she herself had only discovered that Professor Lyne was ill about an hour before. Meanwhile a swab moved dexterously and the needle went in.

'He's a tough, obstinate customer and as proud as Lucifer,' the doctor declared on a note of exasperation and grudging respect. 'He'll go on driving himself until he drops. Fortunately this seems to be a comparatively mild flare-up, and he should pull himself out of it. Has he been under exceptional pressure lately?'

'Well ... we've been working flat out on the book, and he's planning to move back here and start work at the Institute in a couple of weeks.'

'Back to the treadmill. Late sessions, cigar smoke, no proper food and central heating turned up high enough to stupefy the strongest constitution.' The doctor glared at Amelia as if it were her fault.

Remembering that she had abstractedly put all Donovan's clothes away and emptied his grip, Amelia said hesitantly, 'If you're moving the professor to hospital I'll ask the porter to show you where the telephone is and—and get his clothes packed again.'

'He's over the worst, but he'll need nursing for a few more days.' The doctor scrutinised her with pale, rather piercing blue eyes. 'What are you proposing to do?'

'Oh, I shall stay on here,' she said calmly. 'I've arranged for some necessities to be delivered, and I can manage perfectly well until I know how the professor is and what he wishes me to do.'

'Could you manage for both of you?' he demanded unexpectedly.

'You mean ... ?' She met his gaze, and his eyes were much kindlier.

'I don't see any reason to move him, provided there's someone here to look after him and attend to his needs. I could, of course, arrange for a professional nurse for a week or so.'

'I took care of my father for months,' Amelia asserted, 'I think I can cope.'

'So do I, as a matter of fact. You look practical and capable, if I may say so, Miss Leigh, and Donovan is—er—accustomed to you.'

She was so light-headed with relief that the professor was not as desperately ill as her overwrought mind had assumed that she gave the the doctor her glowing smile. 'Tell me exactly what you want me to do.'

He grunted. 'I warn you, he's an intractable patient.'

'Not with me, I'm sure he'll co-operate,' she asserted with unruffled confidence.

'That's what I thought,' was the cryptic reply as he turned to his medical case and began shaking some capsules from a bottle into a small phial. 'I've given him a shot which will deal with the fever. That should see him through the rest of the night. Sponge him down, plenty of fluids to drink, and keep him covered. Give him a couple of these capsules if he shows any signs of distress again.' He snapped his case shut. 'If I know Donovan Lyne he'll be sufficiently recovered tomorrow to be restive and difficult, but he'll have to take it easy for three or four days. No nonsense about the book or the Institute or anything else. Be resolute, Miss Leigh, that's an order. I'll look in again at about midday tomorrow.'

And with that he stalked out, and Amelia followed at a little run to catch up with him at the door. 'Well, Amelia—may I call you Amelia?' he thrust out his hand and shook hers briskly. 'I don't anticipate any more trouble now. Except for you,' a chuckle rumbled through him. 'I've seen him charm and browbeat experienced nurses into getting his own way if he sets his mind to it, so take it steady. Goodbye.'

A little dazed, but with a much lighter heart, Amelia closed the door behind her and leaned against it for a second. Then, making sure all was well in the bedroom, she went into the kitchen. Her purchases were set out on the scarlet formica table top, and it did not take her long to get herself organised. Stacked away in one of the units she found crockery, cutlery and pots and pans, and once she had set up the camping stove in a safe place she put a kettle on to boil.

There was time now to think rationally. The fright and confusion which she had succeeded in hiding from the others had left her feeling rather tired, but there was work yet to be done and the reassurance of the doctor's being willing to leave Donovan in her care put new spirit into her.

She made some tea and took it into the bedroom. Donovan was lying quiet, but at the sound of the tray he stirred and Amelia lifted him and propped the pillows high about his head and shoulders.

Stooping over him, she asked gently, 'Like a drink?'

'Mmm ...' His eyelids were heavy and there was no recognition in his glance. She held the cup to his lips and when he had drunk it all thirstily she allowed herself to relax for a while, seated comfortably beside him as she enjoyed her own cup. If he had not been ill she could have revelled in the quietness and intimacy.

Reluctantly she finished her tea and rose, putting her lips softly to his brow. It was still hot, but not the burning torment of fever she had felt on his skin before. The gesture had been an unguarded expression of her love and concern, and she was suddenly petrified when his hand came up abruptly and caught one of her wrists in a tight grasp.

'Don ... !' She straightened, looking into his face as she tried to pull away. The heavy-lidded stare was disconcerting, to say the least, and her heart began thudding as his grip tightened unbearably. Had the fever abated enough for him to know who she was? Had her emotional anxiety betrayed her? She tried to look away, but couldn't break from his gaze or his hold on her. A deep frown creased his brows, then

70

gradually cleared as he closed his eyes and slackened his grip.

Amelia stood back. Still breathing unevenly, she removed the extra pillow and eased him down, tucking the blankets round. Picking up the cups, she moved to the door when his voice came wearily: 'Amelia?'

She stopped, her eyes shut for a second. Half turning, she answered 'Yes?' in a soft, level tone.

'Yes,' he echoed with a deep sigh, 'I thought so,' and turned his head into the pillow.

In the kitchen she rinsed the cups with slightly tremulous hands. The twilight had faded, and she found a couple of thick pottery ashtrays and set up candles. There was no doubt that Donovan Lyne had recognised her, had probably heard and comprehended a lot more than either she or the doctor had realised. That comatose appearance had been deceptive—he must often have had to cope with fever when he was out in the jungles, and the fact that he had returned was proof of his tremendous strength of will which conserved his energy while at the same time holding on to consciousness for long enough periods to survive. Not even a raging fever could entirely blunt his mind. All she could hope was that she had not revealed her feelings too blatantly. From now on she would be composed and circumspect, as impersonal as possible, for if she was to look after him properly there must be no embarrassment between them.

Amelia had to call on the indefatigable little porter for his assistance again, and he was only too eager to

71

help, intrigued by the situation in Flat Two which had broken the monotony of his day.

Soon he was plodding downstairs laden with linen and coverings. While he festooned the hot water pipes in his quarters with sheets, pillow cases and towels and put an old-fashioned wooden towel-horse in front of an electric heater to air the blankets and duvet, Amelia rang the Manor House at Whimpleford to say that she would not be returning for a few days. Luckily the butler answered the telephone, so her message was brief, without explanations. No point in phoning Apple Tree Cottage, she reasoned, as Mrs Maggs would not be calling in until the following morning. She toyed with the idea of letting Polly Austin know, but decided that that, too, could wait until the next day. Kindly, voluble Polly would probably descend on them in a flurry of agitation, and the doctor had been explicit in ordering complete rest and quiet.

As she came into the flat again, with the faint glow of the candles from the kitchen throwing wavering shadows into the narrow hallway, Amelia heard sounds of movement and knew an instant's panic. With the blinds still up in the bedroom she could see that the bed was empty, the blankets trailing.

'Don?' Her voice sharpened as she moved into the passage.

He was in the bathroom. She waited outside the door in an agony of indecision and was about to go in when he emerged, swaying and pressing his bare shoulder against the wall as he started to find his way back to bed.

She came out of the shadows. 'Here,' she tucked her own shoulder under his arm, easing his weight. 'Did you call out for me?' she asked matter-of-factly. 'I'm sorry. I just slipped out for a moment to telephone.'

'I can make it ... on my own ... too heavy for you.'

'Save your breath. You're not to do this again—not without my help, Professor. There! You're shivering. You must have something to cover with, even if you insist on getting up,' she said severely, and drew the blankets over him, trying not to show how worried she had been.

To her consternation he pulled her down beside him on the bed.

'You smell nice,' he murmured. 'Your perfume ... always know it's you.'

It was a rather expensive cologne, one she had liked for years and started using again once she had a salary coming in and could afford it. It gave her an absurd little surge of pleasure to know it pleased his senses too, and she rested weakly against him, longing to put her arms around him as she had done when he seemed to be unconscious. Then, just as unceremoniously as he had pulled her over, he pushed her hard from him, as though he could no longer endure her presence.

'Why the hell ... don't you ... go home, Amelia?' he said raspingly.

She stood up immediately, biting her lip. 'I shall stay for as long as Dr Hallow considers it necessary,' she replied primly. 'Now do try and rest for a while, Professor. Please stay put while I get things ready to

73

sponge you down and make the bed up for the night.'

Walking to the window, she released the venetian blind and tugged it down with a snap. No use feeling hurt by his sudden rejection, she told herself as she went to the kitchen and fetched the candles; he was too feverish and drugged to know what he was doing. And yet it *had* hurt, because she had let herself go for a moment. She mustn't let reaction to the tensions of the day upset her now.

By the time the kettle had boiled she had extracted her own small face towel from her case and collected enough warm towels from the porter to carry out the job of sponging the professor, as the doctor had instructed, with an impassive efficiency that would have done a trained nurse credit. Donovan submitted, albeit peevishly, and was even more irritable when she had to roll him from one side to the other to get a sheet across the bed under him. But once she had put clean slips on the pillows and made him really comfortable with fresh coverings he became drowsy and amenable.

He turned his head and looked up at her in the guttering candlelight. The room was very quiet. He sighed and said, almost under his breath: 'Thanks ... for being here ... for everything. I'm an ungrateful brute ...'

Tears smarted behind her eyes. Quickly she stooped, picked up the bowl and towels and hurried out of the room.

Amelia sat alone in the kitchen and forced herself to eat the omelette she had made on the stove. Although she had had nothing but a cup of tea since lunchtime she was not hungry, and curiously not a bit sleepy either; yet as she gazed at the flame, wavering like a tiny orange-gold flower on the dripping candle-wax, and tried to think constructively, her mind was going round in futile circles getting nowhere.

Mechanically she cleaned the omelette pan, washed her plate and polished the stainless steel tops until the candlelight shimmered on them. In the bathroom she stripped and washed as best she could with a small kettle of water, and then slipped on her white brushed nylon nightgown and went in search of a room for herself.

There was a large guest room at the end of the corridor with a bow window overlooking the crescent of gardens behind the apartments. She held the candle high and looked around; the shapes muffled under dust sheets were eerie and the cold air made her shiver, but she cleared the cover off the wardrobe and hung up her clothes, and found the dressing table and laid out her meagre possessions. By tilting the glass towards the window and reflecting the candle in it she had enough light to unpin and brush out her hair with long, soothing strokes. In her white gown, with her pale oval face and her hair down to her shoulders, she looked like a slender, vulnerable ghost.

The guest room was too far from Donovan, and Amelia decided to sleep in an armchair near his bed. There was a large, low lounger in the drawing-room which looked as if it would be too heavy to move, but like everything else in the flat it was a superbly made piece of furniture, gliding easily over the thick pile of the carpets, and she had soon made a place for

CHAPTER SIX

OVER the next two days Amelia improvised a routine for nursing Donovan Lyne that worked well. Apart from the dark stubble on his face and a certain pallor, he improved steadily. The borderline of semi-consciousness had gone, and if his manner was vague and lethargic he was perfectly aware of the situation. So was Amelia, dealing with him with firmness and her usual semblance of detachment, never revealing by a word or look, or even the touch of her hands, how she really felt.

She was up each morning at daylight and in addition to tending Donovan started to clean up the flat, with visible results. Whenever Dr Hallow called he seemed satisfied with the way things were progressing. The rooms were no longer dark and musty, and his patient was always ready for him, comfortably propped round with pillows in a neatly-made bed. Amelia was soon organised enough to be able to offer him coffee, which he accepted with brisk cordiality.

'Well, old chap,' he told Donovan, 'a few more days should do it. Luckily Amelia was here. Not many young women would have been prepared to take over as capably as she has. Hang on to her,' he rumbled jovially, 'or I'll shanghai her into the nursing profession!'

77

Amelia served his coffee in the drawing-room, a long, spacious room with pale olive-green hangings, thick terracotta carpeting and dark green corduroy upholstery. Modern ceramic plaques and copper moulds shone against the off-white walls. Yet for all its luxury it had a bare, disciplined appearance that cried out for the small feminine touches of cushions, flowers and ornaments to complete it and bring it to life. The doctor sat sipping his coffee, encouraging Amelia to talk about herself. Then he put the cup aside and took out his prescription pad.

'Is it all right if I leave him for an hour or so now to do some shopping?' Amelia asked diffidently.

'By all means, a walk and a bit of fresh air will do you good.' His pale, acute blue eyes surveyed her. She felt vaguely uncomfortable and pushed up her spectacles. The doctor tore off the prescription form and handed it to her as he rose. 'By the way, I've pulled a few strings about the gas, electricity and telephone, Amelia. In a day or two I hope things will be easier for you.'

'How kind of you, when there are so many other calls on your time,' she smiled at him gratefully. 'I was going to try and do something about that myself.'

'Ah! Well—thank you for the coffee, my dear young lady,' he said as they walked to the door, then he paused with his hand on the knob. He said 'Hmmm' deep in his chest, nodding his head two or three times as if confirming a point. 'If I may say so, as an old friend of Donovan Lyne, you're the first woman in his life who makes absolute sense to me. I'll be looking in again, and if you should need advice you know the telephone number.'

He stalked off down the stairs leaving Amelia with a heightened colour at his gruff compliment. She returned slowly to the kitchen to prepare a drink for Donovan.

'I must go out for a while.' She put the steaming mug and some plain biscuits on his bedside table, within easy reach. 'May I take the key of the flat?'

He opened his eyes. He was quite lucid, his eyelids narrow and enigmatic. 'Help yourself. Pocket of my car coat ... I think.'

She tried to smile and make a light comment on the doctor's visit, but the constraint she had deliberately fostered between them became worse under that narrowed stare. All she could find to say was: 'I'll see you get them back safely.'

She found his keys in his pocket and, tangled up with them, a slip of paper with a brief scrawl— 'Flowers for Marguerite 20th'. To remind himself ... flowers for Marguerite! She pushed the paper back into his pocket with unnecessary force.

Before going out to the shops she remembered to ring Mrs Maggs at the cottage to tell her that the professor was staying on at his flat, but steered clear of village gossip by omitting to mention that she was staying there too. She was in the process of dialling Polly Austin's number when she stopped. Polly would be sure to ring Marguerite Anderson, and then what? The two of them would be supplanting her soon enough; Polly with her affectionate fussing, and Marguerite with—with other kinds of consolation.

Amelia's mouth set. She had so little time to keep

him to herself, to love and watch over him. A mere handful of days now, for it was unlikely that the professor would return to Whimpleford except to pack up. She put the phone down firmly and went shopping.

Sunday passed very quietly. Donovan was in a state of languor, as if the fever had drained his vitality to a low ebb. He hardly spoke and she had to be infinitely patient in persuading him to eat the dishes she made so carefully to tempt him. In between times Amelia scrubbed and polished and tidied the flat to make it habitable, frequently suppressing unsettling thoughts of what she would have liked to do, the little alterations she might have suggested if this had been her home—*their* home. The home they might have made together.

Early on Monday morning she was suddenly wide awake, almost as though a sixth sense had told her things had changed. Pencils of silvery light filtered in through the venetian blinds and she lay very still, listening to the sparrows on the balconette and the distant clink of the milk float down in the street. After a while she threw back the duvet and uncurled from her cramped position in the armchair, sticking out her long, slim legs and wriggling her toes. Lifting her arms, she pushed her hair up from her neck and shook it free into waves, then stretched luxuriously, the graceful swell of her breasts rising as she arched her back.

As she relaxed and turned her head to see if the professor was all right she met his keen grey glance head on. It went through her like a shock wave. Somehow she knew that he had been watching her for some time, and the sheer intimate intensity of his gaze immobilised her. She became conscious of her flimsy nightdress and tumbled hair, and of a warm flood of secret desire that took her breath away.

Grabbing the edges of the duvet, she pulled it round her and got to her feet in a clumsy way. 'Oh, heavens! I m-must have overslept,' she stammered, feeling along the top of the small table for her spectacles. 'Have you—have you been up long?'

'Long enough,' he said tautly.

'You should've called out to me,' she said more confidently as she slipped on her spectacles and thrust her feet into her slippers. 'Is there anything I can do for you before I dress?'

'You know what I want,' he flung himself over on to his back with a stifled exclamation, 'you know damn well what I want.'

'Tea,' she countered equably, clutching the duvet close as she tried to hide her trembling hands. 'I'll put the kettle on to boil, it shouldn't take long.'

'Tea!' he groaned. 'Oh, my God!'

'Would you prefer coffee?'

'Don't be obtuse,' he snapped.

Amelia retreated to the door, almost stumbling over a corner of the duvet draped tightly around her, breathlessly conscious of her racing pulse.

'Amelia?' Her heart lurched at the soft, persuasive undertone. 'Why do you conceal your beautiful hair rolled up in a knot?'

Self-consciously she gathered it together in a bunch and tucked it well down across one shoulder. 'Because it's more manageable, and anyway, I'm hardly of an age to wear floating young hairstyles.' And without risking any further personal questions she left him.

She washed in the cold, black-and-white tiled bathroom, deep in thought. She knew now what had awakened her this morning. Donovan Lyne's need of her had reached her across the shadowy silence of the room, and her instant uncanny response to it had frightened her. In the guest room she dressed hurriedly and pinned her hair up fiercely and more tightly than usual. She left her face devoid of make-up. It was a kind of defence, not only against him but to reinforce her own moments of weakness.

His resilience was remarkable—only a few hours ago the aftermath of the fever had made him morose and apathetic. Now his recovery was likely to plunge her into problems she had not foreseen. Not the sort of problems the doctor had warned her of and she had so blithely shrugged aside, she reflected wryly.

The kettle was boiling merrily on the Primus while Amelia bungled about the kitchen. She accidentally knocked the teapot against the table and dropped the teaspoons with a resounding clatter. She must pull herself together! A virile man's consuming need for a woman was not necessarily concerned with love. Why had fate lured her into loving this particular man? *This* man, who had so casually offered her a temporary refuge in his home and his bed because it suited him. Sensible Amelia Leigh who wouldn't fuss over trivialities or indulge in romantic fantasies! Well, here she was, her feeble nature crying out to share the passion and tenderness she felt for him.

And what good would that do her for the rest of her life?

She bent half over the table, eyes shut tight, overwhelmed with bitterness. She thought she heard a sound at the door and straightened up stiffly, but when she finally carried the tray into the bedroom Donovan was propped up in bed. Intuitively she sensed a difference.

He said abruptly: 'Amelia, I don't know how to thank you for all you've done these last few days.'

'I'm used to nursing,' she replied stiltedly, putting the tray across his knees.

'All the same, it must have been hard going. A sick man in an unused flat without any amenities,' his jaw tightened. 'Quite a strain for you.'

She walked round and swished up the venetian blinds, flooding the room with sunlight. 'Oh, Dr Hallow's been a great help. It will all be functioning soon—today or tomorrow with a bit of luck. The kettle's on again and as soon as you've finished your tea I'll help you wash and freshen up, Professor.'

'Put the kettle in the bathroom for me,' he requested curtly.

A flicker of anxiety broke the blankness of her expression. 'Do you think you should get up? Only yesterday you were——'

'Do as I ask, please, Amelia.'

His tone was so final and uncompromising that the protest died on her lips. It was no use quoting the doctor to him. She made herself scarce, tidying up the bathroom and calling out to him when everything was ready. His mood had altered decisively and she was helpless against it.

Nevertheless her heart was in her mouth all the while he was splashing in the bathroom. As she made up the bed she kept glancing at the door, and as she replaced her armchair in its original position in the drawing room she heard the drone of his electric shaver. A loud expletive, strong and earthy, was more reassuring to her ears. The professor was himself again—no doubt about that. But with it came the realisation that Amelia's days with him, those precious days of tending and brooding over him, were pretty well over. And her days of working with him as his assistant were numbered.

Contrary to Dr Hallow's predictions he was a model patient after that, except for an immovable determination to do everything possible for himself. The workmen arrived, clumped cheerfully about, adjusted meters and switches and restored the telephone connection. The doctor spent shorter periods in rumbling conversation with his patient, patted Amelia on the shoulder and told her she must come and have dinner with his wife and himself, to which she responded with a rather wooden, noncommittal smile. And all the while the atmosphere of constraint in the flat grew until it had become a painful, perplexing estrangement.

Amelia spent most of her time now in cleaning, shopping and preparing meals, carrying a tray into Donovan's bedroom and offering one lame excuse after another for having her own meal in the kitchen. He made no attempt to dissuade her, commenting sardonically: 'Go ahead, my dear girl, it's more convenient than eating off the corner of my bedside table.' She fetched him books and newspapers, when he asked for them, but conversation between them had virtually ceased, and each evening she would escape, swallowing her tears, to the guest room which she now occupied, half packed, like a transient guest in a hotel.

It was on Thursday morning, when she overheard him on the telephone extension arranging with someone at the Institute to go down to Whimpleford to pack up his papers and personal belongings, that she saw with agonising clarity what lay ahead. So he did not intend to go himself ... or ask her help! It was spring—but for Amelia Leigh the year was over.

That night Amelia came to a decision. She had promised Emma that she would not be an encumbrance at the Manor House again. She had broken through the inertia which had held her in Whimpleford, and if Donovan was not returning, there was nothing for her to do there. In fact there was no need for her to return to Whimpleford at all. She ought to be grateful to Donovan Lyne. He had roused her dormant emotions, absorbed her into his interests, turned her old life upside down. And in the past few days he had slowly but surely succeeded in convincing her that the time had come for her to make her own way. As soon as he was fit enough to fend for himself, that was precisely what she would do.

She lay in one of the twin beds in the guest room of the flat trying to make plans for a still nebulous future. She remembered that on her way to the Fenn Institute for an appointment that never materialised, she had seen the name-plate of an employment agency which looked quiet and discreet; and on the drive back in the cab she recalled the name of a small bed-and-breakfast hotel which might suit her as a temporary *pied-à-terre*. It seemed like a lifetime ago, although it was only a week. Here, at least, were two points of reference in such a large city that she would be able to find again, and she eventually fell asleep reassuring herself that she could manage on her own quite well.

The next morning she should have felt bright and active, now that she had made up her mind; but her decision to cut clean from Donovan Lyne and from her home in Whimpleford at one and the same time weighed on her spirits like a dull ache.

To her surprise, when she emerged from the kitchen with the professor's breakfast tray, she found him already up and dressed writing at the desk in his study. This was the one place that, apart from dusting, she had not attempted to tidy up. The broad sunlit room was overflowing with books and papers, and where the crowded bookshelves ended the walls were decorated with carved and feathered aboriginal masks, lethal-looking spears and painted shields. Even the top of the window ledge was loaded with ritual objects, lumps of volcanic lava and fragments of bone.

She rested the tray gingerly on the corner of the desk. He looked up and thanked her with a preoccupied smile.

'Are you—do you feel up to this yet?' she ventured a trifle anxiously.

The smile disappeared. His eyes were seeking something as he looked steadily at her pallid face. She made a business of pushing up and adjusting her spectacles to avoid this uncomfortable scrutiny.

He said: 'I'm fine now. Much quicker than I would otherwise have been, thanks to your ministrations, Amelia.' He got up and moved restlessly to the window, rubbing his hand over the back of his neck and easing his shoulders. 'I wish I could say your *devoted* care!' He gave a short, jarring laugh.

Hurt by what she took to be sarcasm, she turned blindly towards the door. He called, 'I'm sorry, Amelia, I don't know why I said that. Put it down to the frustrations of convalescence. Have you had breakfast? Can you spare me a minute?'

'Well, I—I have to go shopping, and I must speak to the porter.'

'This won't take long.' He reached for his briefcase and extracted his cheque book. 'Please sit down,' he said in a quiet, almost weary tone.

But she remained standing, wiping all expression from her face as she watched him return to the desk and write out a cheque.

He said in the same precise, level voice: 'I cannot allow you to work in the flat as a combined nurse, cook and cleaner any longer. And I haven't paid your salary this month either.'

She took the cheque from him with nerveless fingers. She would rather have died than betray the pain his words had inflicted, but the amount made out to her took her breath away.

'But this isn't my salary, you've made a mistake——'

'No mistake,' he swivelled his chair away to look out of the window, his back to her. 'Please accept it, Amelia. I want you to have it. You've worked selflessly for me for months, and in this last week I couldn't have managed without you. A professional nurse would have cost as much, probably more. Think of it as a bonus. I want you to go back to Whimpleford and have a break for a while. Spend it on clothes and having a good time—a bit of a holiday somewhere. You deserve it.'

'For services rendered,' she murmured bitterly under her breath.

'I've had a word on the phone with Polly Austin, she and Bill are coming over later today.' He took a cigarette from his case. The sunlight showed the drawn lines on his bony face, and his knuckles were white gripping the lighter. 'Why didn't you ring and let Polly know the way I've been imposing on you?' he asked awkwardly. Then, without waiting for her to reply: 'Polly thinks she can get hold of a capable woman to take on the housekeeping of the flat until I can make other arrangements. It isn't fair to tie you down. You look as if you could do with a rest.'

'Oh,' she said, staring at the cheque, 'if you say so ...' She felt too stupefied to find anything else to say now that the moment had come. She was being paid off. She backed towards the door.

'Polly and Bill are looking forward to meeting you again,' he added.

'Yes.' Her throat was dry. 'Well, thank you for your generous cheque. Will you excuse me? I have a lot to do.'

'Amelia?' She paused at the door as he spoke, without turning. 'I'll never be able to express my appreciation for all you've done.'

'Oh, but you have!' she returned in a dead voice, and held up the cheque. Fifteen minutes later she put a brief farewell note, together with the keys of the flat, on his bedside table. He was still in his study. Case in hand, she crossed the hall and quietly let herself out.

CHAPTER SEVEN

DONOVAN Lyne would never know what he had accomplished with the cheque he had given her, thought Amelia. That small piece of paper had severed their relationship with the sharp, clean, agonising cut of a knife. He could not have made his lack of feeling clearer.

What had she expected? For her, looking after him had been a secret outpouring of love, letting her patience and concern speak for her; if she had agreed to marry him he would no doubt have accepted her help without question. But he probably felt under an obligation which had become more and more irksome until he could stand it no longer.

What hurt most was that he had made no attempt to talk things over, even as friends. He knew she had no wish to return to Whimpleford. He knew she was hoping for his help in finding something suitable in London. Instead he had proffered a cheque and told her to go home.

If she had not needed that cheque to get her through the next few weeks she would have torn it up and thrown it on his desk. A silly gesture, she reflected sadly, which would have succeeded in angering and embarrassing him while it only relieved her feelings temporarily.

For two days Amelia walked in the void she had been dreading, doing mechanically what had to be done. Having opened a bank account with the professor's cheque she was able to book into a small hotel in Bayswater as the usual influx of overseas tourists had not yet begun to crowd into London. She felt guilty at not having phoned Polly Austin, particularly when Donovan was ill, but to do so now would require explanations she was not prepared to give. Nor did she wish to renew a contact which would inevitably draw her back into the professor's circle. As far as he was concerned she had gone back to Whimpleford, and she wanted it to stay that way.

On the third day, after spending most of her time sitting listlessly in her small hotel, Amelia made a determined effort to pull herself together. She dressed carefully in the new outfit she had bought in Whimpleford, called a taxi and gave the name of the employment bureau she had noticed on the way to Donovan's flat. It would have been cheaper on a double-decker bus, but she was not yet sufficiently sure of her way around town.

The cab took her to Great Russell Street. She paid it off at the corner of Museum Street and walked the short distance, straightening her coat and pushing up her spectacles nervously. She was prepared to take whatever job they offered her. Without giving herself a chance to hesitate she pushed open the glass door and walked in.

It was a long, narrow office with three desks and some lounge chairs, and a rack of decorative pot plants patterning one wall. At one desk a thin, very precisely dressed man was interviewing a girl. The second desk was empty. From the third a woman rose and smilingly beckoned Amelia forward.

'Do you have an appointment?'

'No, I'm sorry,' Amelia said awkwardly. 'I didn't realise it was necessary for a preliminary inquiry about getting work.'

'Preferable, but not necessary.' The woman's dark, rather prominent eyes swept over Amelia, leaving the impression that she had weighed up the possibilities in one shrewd glance. 'Come in and sit down, Miss—er——'

'Leigh. Amelia Leigh.'

'Miss Leigh.' Her hand was soft but her handshake was brief and firm. 'I'm Hannah Hall. I have a number of girls to see this morning, and calls to make, but the first appointment is not for another fifteen minutes or so, time enough for us to have a talk.' She drew out a large index card and opened her pen as Amelia sat down opposite her.

'Now, perhaps a few preliminary details?'

The bare, prosaic facts about her went down on the card. This was interrupted by a telephone call which gave Amelia a chance to watch the older woman. She must have been in her fifties, with a rather florid complexion; in a black overdress with white lace at collar and wrists, heavy rings on long manicured fingers and an immaculate arrangement of dark wavy hair. Their eyes met for a second and the woman smiled again, and for some inexplicable reason Amelia felt reassured and much more confident about the prospects.

When the card had been completed, Hannah Hall began probing so skilfully and sympathetically that Amelia found herself giving a candid account of her life—all but the past ten days.

'Professor Lyne, did you say? Donovan Lyne? I remember reading about him, a very distinguished anthropologist. And something else about him,' she added musingly. 'I can't think for the moment what it was.' She paused. 'That's beside the point. Do you think Professor Lyne would give you a reference?'

'I'm sure he would,' Amelia agreed haltingly, 'but ... but if it's possible without bothering him ...'

Hannah Hall noted the reluctance, thinking: she's in love with him and she's followed him to London and doesn't want him to know yet. She said briskly, 'Well, we shall have to see. Any other references?'

'There's my old tutor at college. And the vicar and the doctor in Whimpleford. I suppose you would call those character references. But I'm quite willing to take a typing test, or work on some project without pay until I've proved myself.'

'Hmm.' Hannah Hall studied Amelia silently for a few moments. 'You're going to be difficult to place,' —Amelia's heart sank—'your background is too good to waste on filing or copy-typing. We don't handle much at that level anyway. Don't look so disappointed!' she went on bracingly. 'We're developing a service for literary and general research assistants, and you might fit into something later. Meanwhile,' she pursed her coral-red lips in thought, 'how would you like to start by working in this office? My husband and I, and my nephew, run the agency between us, but my nephew has had a bout of 'flu, so there's a vacancy here at the moment.'

Amelia blinked. 'But I know nothing about interviewing and placing!'

'Then I shall teach you a few of the techniques. Common sense is a prime commodity; I think you have it, and we shall soon test your judgement.'

'If you really feel I could cope ...'

'I do.' Hannah Hall named a salary which was more than Amelia had dared to hope for at this early stage. 'When can you start?'

'Whenever you wish.'

'Good. Take off your coat—I think a useful beginning would be for you to sit in on my interviews today, and we can take it from there.'

Hannah Hall led her out to the staff rooms at the back of the office where she left Amelia to hang up her coat, tidy her hair and add a touch of lipstick to her pale mouth. She was astonished at her good fortune—that of all the agencies in London she should have noticed this place, and that they had offered her something immediately, however temporary. She liked Hannah Hall, she would have a chance to show her capabilities and she would be on the spot should any other opportunities turn up. It was too good to be true, she thought with the first little spurt of elation she had felt since those small signs of improvement in Donovan Lyne while she was nursing him. Was it only last week?

How was he now? Had Polly Austin filled the gap she had created so abruptly? As the memories threatened to sweep over her again she pushed them determinedly into her subconscious and went out to join Hannah Hall at her desk and involve herself in other people's problems.

In the weeks that followed Amelia had no time for introspection, at least during working hours, and as the bright evenings lengthened she had a chance to explore some of London's byways. She would stroll down through Lincoln's Inn Fields under the graceful trees, perhaps stop for a moment to watch the tennis enthusiasts on the courts, then out, past the venerable red brick walls behind which many eminent lawyers had their chambers, and across Carey Street to the gothic arches and turrets of the Law Courts, looking for all the world like a Ruritanian palace but built for much sterner purposes.

Standing on the traffic island at Temple Bar she could look down Fleet Street with its crowded pavements and its close-packed buildings bearing the names of famous newspapers, and beyond them, soaring in the distance, the magnificent dome of St Paul's on Ludgate Hill; while to her right the statue of Dr Samuel Johnson stood below the sheltering east window of St Clement Dane's, known to children all over the world for its peal of bells which rang out the rhyme of 'Oranges and Lemons'.

Sometimes she would complete her pilgrimage by going across to the arch which led into the Temple, another stronghold of the legal profession, and walking down through the Temple gardens, the traditional scene of the plucking of the red and white roses which became the emblems of the bloody and bitter struggle for the throne between the Houses of Lancaster and York in the Wars of the Roses. The lower gate led out on to the Embankment, where the evening sun hung like a scarlet ball over the Thames and touched with gold the graceful arches of Waterloo Bridge and the rippling tide of the powerful old river.

Here Amelia could feel in her bones a deep sense of continuity and history, of triumphs and of sorrows which made her own heartache and despondency seem trivial by comparison. Refreshed by the pungent breeze and the cool pink and grey wash of the sunset sky, she would return up one of the narrow streets to the Strand and join the throngs jostling for buses to get home.

Home for her was still a hotel room, a case with a few clothes and no personal possessions at all. She knew she must arrange about her few belongings at the Manor House in Whimpleford, but there was nowhere to store them yet. She could not stay at the hotel indefinitely, for she could not afford the high season rates. This came home to her more sharply when the manager asked courteously if she were prolonging her visit, as he already had bookings for the season which included her room.

Lying on her bed, overwhelmed by loneliness, she pondered the difficulty of finding a bed-sitter within her means. The easy answer would have been to ring Polly Austin; her eager offer had been genuine at the time, but she might well be feeling differently about Amelia now, and Amelia shrank from the thought of approaching her.

She eventually decided to ask Hannah Hall for advice. She and her husband Charles had been more than kind, but never intrusive about Amelia's life outside the office. They were perfect foils for each other, Hannah with her flamboyant chic and shrewd eyes, and Charles very gaunt and precise, with meticulous manners. Neither had tried to force Amelia's confidence, confining their interest to her work, which she carried out serenely and conscientiously as she knew how. She had met the Halls' nephew, who was due to return shortly from a convalescent holiday in the South of France.

This was another point Amelia knew she must raise with the Halls; thus the question of where to live and the question of future employment came at the same time to oppress her with new doubts. As for Donovan Lyne—he haunted her wakeful thoughts at night. Was he well? Had he missed her enough to inquire at Whimpleford? Would he have made any attempt to find her if he knew? She longed to glimpse the strong-boned angular face again, to watch his restless expressive hands, to turn to him and shed completely her desperate loneliness and her problems.

On the Friday morning Hannah, who had been opening the mail, called Amelia over and handed her a letter. It was from a well-known Park Lane hotel. The writer, an American, said that he had been recommended to the agency by a fellow American who had used their services the previous year. He would be in England for three months searching for old documents concerning his family among parochial and provincial records, and required a com-

97

petent person in London to transcribe his notes and do some research for him at the Public Record Office.

Amelia looked up from the letter, hardly daring to show her eagerness until she met Hannah's smile.

Hannah said: 'This has come at the right time, hasn't it? Max, my nephew, will be back some time next week. I'm sure you can tackle it, Amelia, you can learn as you go along, as you've done here with us.' She looked at the girl's flushed cheeks and suddenly animated expression, thinking that this was preferable to the pallor and the smudges she had seen under Amelia's eyes whenever she removed her spectacles for a few minutes.

'Is it a reprieve, Amelia?' she laughed briefly.

'No, of course not!' Amelia retorted. 'I've enjoyed being here, meeting people and being kept busy all day. But I was rather concerned about what was going to happen when your nephew returned.'

'Well, that's settled, then. Let's ring this Mr Harry B. Barnes and arrange an appointment for you.'

'Hannah,' Amelia hesitated for a moment, 'there was something else I wanted to ask you, and it's rather pressing with the possibility of this three-month commission.'

'Ask away. If it's something Charles and I can advise you about, we will.'

'I can't go on staying at a hotel—they have the season's bookings starting now. I've tried all the small ads. in the papers, and the offers of accommodation on stationers' shops, but I haven't found anything yet.'

'I wondered how you were managing,' said Hannah reflectively, 'finding accommodation is so difficult in town. How long have you got?'

'Another week. They might stretch it to two.'

'Let me think it over, and I'll ask around.'

'Thanks. I'll keep on searching too.' Amelia pushed up her spectacles and smoothed back her hair. 'I'd better ring Mr Barnes right away.'

She bought a new two-piece, a dress in navy-and-white tweed jersey with a buttoned jacket, and a head-hugging white hat and matching accessories, and as she caught a bus to Marble Arch and walked down Park Lane she could feel the soft, restless touch of April. She was ushered up to see the American visitor in a suite overlooking Hyde Park. The trees looked almost iridescent as the breeze ruffled the pale young leaves with sunlight. There were distant splashes of colour in formal flower borders, the silvery glint of the Serpentine, and smooth undulating greens.

Harry B. Barnes, small and spiky like an alert terrier, was surprisingly easy to talk to; as he spoke of his plans for visiting towns and villages his small eyes danced with excitement at the thought of what was obviously for him a holiday treasure hunt. He had soon communicated this enthusiasm for delving into old documents to Amelia, and they came to a satisfactory arrangement. She was to type and collate his notes as he completed each part of his search, and also make some searches for him whenever necessary.

Her only regret afterwards was that she had had to mention working with Donovan Lyne. He was very impressed, but as he was leaving London within a couple of days and was full of his own plans, Amelia concluded that he wouldn't take up the reference, much to her relief.

Max Hall returned to the office the next morning just as Amelia was setting off for that ornate grey Victorian castle, the Public Record Office in Chancery Lane. His berry-brown tan accentuated his fair hair and blue eyes. He gave her a wide, impudent grin: 'Off to begin digging up literary fossils? Rather you than me! See you later!'

He was not in the office when she returned at about three to type up her notes for her American employer, but Hannah greeted her: 'Oh good, you're back early. Max has a proposition which might interest you.'

Amelia looked faintly startled and Hannah laughed. 'It's about accommodation—and quite proper, I assure you!'

'So soon? That's wonderful!'

Hannah tilted her head, still looking amused. 'You know, Amelia, there's something about that calm, well-balanced air of yours that shook Max a little. Although he's quite capable of mischief if he sets his mind to it, so be warned!'

Amelia nodded with a light laugh. Any prospect of finding somewhere to live sounded hopeful, even if it came from that rangy young man with the predatory twinkle in his blue eyes.

As they were having a break, drinking tea, he walked in and was formally introduced. 'Amelia Leigh? What a mouthful! How about making it Amy or Melly?'

100

'Make it Amelia.'

'Amelia, lord save us! Down, boy! The lady's on her dignity.'

'You're absurd!' she smiled unselfconsciously, and his blue eyes widened with a sudden awareness.

'Hannah says you may know of a place I can live?' she enquired.

'Yep, there's this mate of mine whose parents have a pad in the City. Used to be the porter's flat in a block of offices—they might let a nice girl like you have a couple of rooms. Mind you, it's pretty damn quiet in the City after the commuters go home.'

'The city?' she repeated, puzzled.

'The old City of London, country girl. The original square mile within the sound of Bow Bells, where the banks and insurance companies and other financial wizards have their being now. That's the City—the bit here is the West End, or just "town". We'll make a good cockney of you yet!'

'Can you arrange for me to meet those people?' she asked.

'What's it worth?' He gave her a quick grin. 'Will you have dinner with me?'

'When?' she asked dubiously.

'What's wrong with after work tonight? Unless you have a date.'

'No, I haven't, and I'd like to get something settled soon, if I can. So, if you can spare the time——'

'I'll check with my social secretary and put off the numerous other beautiful dollies waiting for me to do them a good turn.'

This time Amelia couldn't resist laughing out loud.

She turned to Hannah, who threw up her hands. 'He means it, Amelia. Disregard the rest of his nonsense.'

'Sure I mean it,' Max declared. 'I'll give the old chap a ring and find out if they can see us this evening. If they can, fine—if they can't it's still a date tonight, Amelia?'

'All right, thank you, Max,' she conceded, liking him for all his brashness, and wondering how long it would be before the novelty of countrified Amelia Leigh would wear off and he was back with his London girl-friends. He was the type to 'play the field', as Edward would have said, and irresistibly good-humoured.

Max took her to the hub of the City, between the Bank of England and the Mansion House, then along a crowded street and through an archway into a quiet courtyard where the sound of the rush hour traffic faded. The flat was semi-basement down a shallow flight of stairs.

The Clarks welcomed them at the door, and Max introduced her to the elderly couple. 'Max,' the woman scolded, 'why don't you come and see us more often? Brian is always asking after you in his letters. My son,' she explained to Amelia, 'he's posted to Brussels at present. It's his corner we're thinking of letting.'

They all went into a rather heavily furnished parlour where they sipped sherry and chatted for a while. Amelia was aware she was being subjected to a discreet interrogation but took it in good part, and knew she had been accepted when Mrs Clark offered to show her the accommodation. It was a fairly large room, part furnished as a sitting room and the rest partitioned off as a small bedroom. There was a fitted wash-bowl and the bathroom was just along the narrow corridor outside. Amelia was surprised to find that the inner windows of the flat looked out on an area railing enclosing a tiny garden, with a tree and some grass and tubs of flowering shrubs, a green seclusion hidden among the solid office blocks.

'We wouldn't normally let,' Mrs Clark confided as she showed Amelia the small neat kitchen they would share, 'but as you're a friend of Charles and Hannah Hall, I think we shall get on well together.'

'May I bring a few of my own things for my room?' Amelia asked.

'Of course. It doesn't feel homely until one has a few bits and pieces of one's own, does it?'

When they discussed terms it was arranged for Amelia to move in at the weekend. Once again she could scarcely believe her good luck; her spirits rose and she was determined to enjoy the rest of the evening. Max had not brought his car because of the many parking problems, so they went down to the Bank underground station and took the tube.

They had dinner in a restaurant near Holborn. Max was such a boyishly light-hearted companion that Amelia began to relax, accepting his gossipy conversation and tall tales with amused indulgence, quite unaware that he was watching the difference in her, the faint colour in her pale cheeks, the gentle humour, the gradual shedding of some of her reserve.

It was not until the waiter had brought their coffee and a brandy for Max that he suddenly leaned across the table towards her and fixed her with a bold, appraising stare. 'You know, Amelia,' he said reflectively, 'if you changed to a softer hair-style, and wore delicate fly-away frames instead of those goldfish-bowl glasses, you'd be the most stunning girl I know.'

A shutter came down on her pleasure as she pushed the offending spectacles with the tip of her finger. 'Max, it's been a wonderful evening, don't spoil it by becoming personal.'

'Why should becoming personal spoil it? I'm a person, you're a person. I'm interested in you as a person. You have a skin like peaches, a sweet little nose, a charming oval face, a good figure—whenever anyone gets a chance to look at it with those staid clothes! And your eyes,' he reached out and removed the hornrims before she could stop him, 'are beautiful.'

She hastily put down her coffee cup. 'Please, Max!'

'Amelia, how old are you?'

She took the spectacles from him and replaced them, saying coldly: 'It's none of your business, but I'm twenty-five.'

'Is that all? I'm a couple of years older than you, but you've been looking at me and treating me as though you were a tolerant maiden aunt! You know your trouble, you take life too seriously.'

'I take it as I've found it,' she returned.

'No fripperies, no fun? What gives with you?' He sat back. 'Some man, I'll bet!'

'No,' she protested, too swiftly and untruthfully.

'Hannah said you've been working for the past year for this professor. Was he a dull, desiccated stick who trimmed all the joy out of you?'

'He was neither dull nor desiccated,' she said indignantly. 'Really, Max, you're impossible! Please stop this silly conversation.'

He looked sulky for a moment, then sighed theatrically. 'Okay, Miss Amelia Leigh. Maybe I should mind my own business, but it's going to be tough. Like some more coffee?'

When she refused he paid the bill, helped her into her coat and gave her shoulders a brief tap. 'If you'll let me see you home I promise not to trespass again,' he grinned. 'Not tonight, anyway.'

Still feeling a little ruffled at his outspokenness, she thanked him for the dinner in a polite little voice, and they came out into the soft violet twilight of the lengthening day. Max took her arm and shepherded her down the street to cross at the traffic lights to the underground station.

They stood for a few seconds on the curb waiting for the lights to change. As the orange flickered to red a car pulled up sharply beside them and in one stupefied moment Amelia saw the angular profile which could stop her heart. Donovan Lyne turned his head, looking directly at her, and it was like a physical collision. The incredulity in his expression and gradual tightening of his lips sent the blood pulsing through her, and she stood by the bumper of the low grey coupé as if her feet were rooted to the crossing.

Max Hall pulled at her arm. 'Hey, Amelia! The lights are changing. Come on.' He hustled her over the crossing just in time. She craned her neck for one more desperate glimpse of Don, but the car accelerated and was hidden by the traffic. He must have recognised her, just as she had recognised him at once, even in the half-light. She suddenly remembered that the Fenn Foundation was somewhere near here, in a square off Holborn; in the jumble of her thoughts she told herself she must avoid this area at all costs in future.

The crowded entrance to the station was a kind of bolt-hole into which she could disappear, in case Donovan Lyne turned his car and came back. It was she who was in a hurry now. Max faced her under the fluorescent lighting of the escalator and said anxiously: 'Are you ill, Amelia? you're looking very pale ... don't pass out on me, will you, sweetie?'

'Sorry, Max,' she said limply. 'I'm rather tired, just take me home.'

CHAPTER EIGHT

THE Saturday Amelia went back to Whimpleford to retrieve her personal possessions, it poured with rain. The City was wet, grey and half empty in the early morning as she walked to Moorgate and took a train to Paddington station.

Shortly after leaving Donovan Lyne's flat, she had written to Emma explaining that she had decided to stay in London permanently, and giving her the name of her bank to write to until she had a settled address. Emma's exasperated reply demanded to know where she had been all this time; and what had become of that supercilious anthropologist? And if she didn't come down soon to collect the things she had left behind, one of the local charities would be glad enough to have them for a jumble sale. Ruefully Amelia reflected that her sister seemed less concerned for her welfare than piqued about not being kept informed.

Once she had moved in with the Clarks she sent Emma another note telling her she would be returning to the Manor House for a couple of days to clear up her old room. Max Hall offered to drive her in his car, but she refused on the grounds that he would be at a loose end while she was busy packing, and she didn't want any distractions.

'Excuses, excuses,' he teased with a grin. 'Have you a lover hidden away in this rural retreat?'

'Dozens of them,' she laughed lightly. 'They'll be lining the road to welcome me back.'

As she changed from the local platform to the main line Amelia had to admit to herself that she did not want to be seen in the village with Max Hall in tow; the kindly but inveterate gossips would talk too much. But he had been so determined that she had had to agree to his coming to fetch her back on Sunday afternoon. Dear Max! If it had not been for his amusing and persistent attentions in the last couple of weeks she might have given way to the despondency which had tormented her since she saw Donovan Lyne again. As it was, the chance of another unexpected encounter had kept her alert and edgy for days; part of her longed to meet Donovan, part of her dreaded the possibility.

She put her case on the rack, shook out her damp raincoat and sank into a corner seat of the compartment. Her only companions were a stout woman and a young girl. The train pulled slowly away and snaked out through the rail yards, past the back gardens of the suburbs and on towards the open countryside.

Amelia sighed; she was not looking forward to these two days. She took off the pretty silk square of scarf and ran her fingers up through the soft waves of her hair. That was another of Max's achievements, she thought, persuading her to go to an extremely expensive hairdresser to have it restyled. Taking the compact from her bag, she flipped open the mirror. In all fairness, the way the man had cut it, shortening and reshaping it into a graceful curve about her neck, had made an extraordinary difference—not only was it easier to manage and flattering to her face, but it had given her a psychological lift when she badly needed it. Perhaps she would take Max's advice in changing the shape of her spectacles too. Tucking the compact away, she pulled out a book and became immersed in it for the rest of the journey.

When the train eventually rolled into Whimpleford station the familiar sights and sounds swept over her in a wave of nostalgia. The clouds had been left behind and the sun was shining. She slipped on the fashionable raincoat, knotted her scarf round the handle of her bag, lifted her case down and stepped, bare-headed, out into the sunshine.

She smiled brightly at the ticket collector who had known her since her college days, but the weeks in London must have altered her appearance and manner more than she realised, for he didn't recognise her at first. Then he smiled back broadly and asked if she had come for a holiday.

'Just a couple of days,' Amelia said.

'A bit of quiet after London, eh, Miss Amelia? Next bus to Whimpleford isn't till eleven o'clock.'

'Yes, I know. I think I'll take a taxi from Market Square.'

Driving up the sweep of the Manor House drive to the flight of shallow steps, she couldn't help remembering the last time—getting so happily into the car beside Donovan, breathing the first whiff of freedom, little realising how much those moments were going to alter her life. Vague qualms about Emma's inevitable inquisition filled her as she paid off the taxi and watched it drive away.

The butler opened the door and welcomed her warmly; Amelia had always been considerate, and very popular with the servants. He ushered her into the high-ceilinged, gold and white entrance hall and was helping her off with her coat when Emma came languidly down the curving staircase in a long house-gown of embroidered silk. For a few seconds she looked surprised as she surveyed the town gloss on her younger sister, the London clothes, the make-up used sparingly but effectively, and a new air of confidence that was difficult to define.

'You've changed, Melly, even in this short time.' She walked over and gave her a perfunctory peck on the cheek. 'Bring us some coffee to the drawing-room, Haskins,' she called to the butler who was taking Amelia's coat and case up to her room. As soon as the butler was out of earshot she turned and said peevishly, 'The trouble you've caused, Melly!'

'Trouble?' Amelia followed her into the panelled room with its sporting prints, disheartened to think that the recriminations had started already. 'Isn't it convenient for me to collect my things this weekend? You didn't write or phone to say no.'

'Oh, that,' Emma shrugged. 'The sooner you clear out your junk the better. I want to give your room to one of the maids. She's sharing at the moment. The club's doing so well, and with the summer on top of us we've had to increase the staff.'

'I won't get in your way, Emma. Pickfords will be

picking up my trunk and Grandmother's old rocking chair on Monday morning, and that will be the last you need bother about me.'

'Oh, will it, indeed! And what about Professor Lyne?'

Disconcerted by the sudden question, Amelia sank into an armchair. 'What about him? I'm not working for him now, I'm doing research for a visiting American at the moment.'

'For heaven's sake,' Emma flounced into a chair opposite, 'you might have told us!'

'I wrote and told you I had another job,' said Amelia uncomfortably.

'Only this week. What have you been up to? Professor Lyne telephoned out of the blue a fortnight ago asking to speak to you. He seemed to think you should be here—it was most embarrassing.'

The arrival of the butler with the coffee service ended Emma's strictures for a few minutes, giving Amelia time to pull herself together before the next onslaught. He waited for Emma to pour, carried her cup to Amelia, proffered a silver dish of biscuits and when Amelia declined returned it to the salver and quietly withdrew.

'I find Professor Lyne very unpleasant when he talks in that abrupt, intimidating voice, as if he were speaking to one of his underlings.' Emma picked up her coffee cup, bridling at the recollection. 'He was quite annoyed when I told him you'd stayed in London, and didn't he know? He said angrily if he had known he wouldn't have been phoning. His tone was

111

most offensive.' Her eyes narrowed. 'Did you walk out on him?'

'No ... yes, in a way, I suppose.' Amelia turned away, sipping her coffee.

'What does that mean?' Emma's sharp white teeth bit into a biscuit.

'I'd finished all the work I could do for him,' Amelia told her guardedly. 'He expected me to return here, but I—I took another job instead.'

She calculated quickly in her mind that Donovan Lyne must have telephoned after seeing her that night with Max. He had no right to be angry because she had refused to run obediently back to Whimpleford on his orders! Not after the indifferent way he had practically dismissed her.

'Why on earth didn't you tell him you'd found another job?' Emma complained crossly. 'We couldn't even tell him where you were living at that time. Heaven knows what all the fuss was about, but he insisted that we let him know as soon as we heard from you, and Edward felt it his duty to give him your address and tell him that you were coming down today.'

'You mean,' Amelia couldn't help murmuring, '*you* felt it was Edward's duty.' So now Donovan knew where to find her in London, she thought.

'Don't quibble! Edward and I were very worried about what you might or might not have done—mislaid the professor's papers, or left something important unfinished. I don't like the man, but it was decent of him to provide you with work for a whole year and take you up to town with him.'

112

'I earned my salary,' Amelia replied quietly, 'and I'm satisfied I did everything that required doing. Whatever was left unfinished was his own decision.'

'I still can't understand all this ridiculous confusion.' Emma was eyeing Amelia with pointed curiosity. 'Edward had a long session with him last evening, but he got nothing out of him.'

Amelia was startled. 'Did he come down here?'

'He *is* here.'

After a slight pause, Amelia asked numbly: 'At the cottage?'

'Here in the Manor. He arrived from London in time for dinner yesterday. He's still a member of the club, or had you forgotten?'

Amelia put her coffee cup down carefully on the table because her hands were so unsteady. 'No, but he seldom used the club.'

'Well, he's using it now, and he wants to see you, so it must be something serious. Do try and think what you could have bungled, Melly, and have some proper answers for him. This hole-and-corner behaviour reflects on Edward and me. Why on earth did you cut yourself off in that melodramatic way?'

'Don't exaggerate, Emma.' It was an effort to try and speak placidly while her mind could only focus on Donovan's presence in the club. 'I assured you I would never be a burden to you again. And I intend to go on as I think fit.' She moved to the edge of her chair, gripped by the need to get away to the refuge of her room. 'If you'll excuse me, I'd like to go upstairs and make a start on my packing.'

'Really, Melly!' Emma clicked her tongue with

exasperation. 'How can you be so casual about everything? Have you no feeling, no concern for others? You're so uncommunicative I could scream! Even when Daddy died——'

'I'd rather not discuss it,' Amelia was stung into retorting. 'I may not be emotional, but I have my feelings.' She got to her feet. 'Where's Edward?'

'He's out playing golf.' Emma rose too and said plaintively: 'Look, I know you think I'm interfering, but we *are* sisters. You never confide in me, you never have, and it's very hurtful.'

'I'm sorry,' Amelia replied. 'I have nothing to confide, Emma, and nothing to be ashamed of, so there's no need for Edward and you to worry on my account.'

They stood looking at each other for a moment, then Emma turned away and shrugged. 'Have it your own way,' she said frustratedly. 'Edward was convinced you and the professor had had a row, but I know you,' she added tartly, 'you couldn't rouse yourself sufficiently to have an argument, let alone a row! You just ran away.'

It was near enough to the truth to make Amelia wince. Speaking as calmly as she could she asked: 'When am I supposed to meet Professor Lyne?'

'Well, he's gone to see Dr Truscott this morning, he seems to know him quite well.'

'Yes, of course.' Amelia felt a stirring of anxiety as to whether it was a professional or merely a social visit; then concluded that it was the latter because he was only here for the weekend.

'He would like you to join him for lunch,' said

114

Emma, 'in the main dining room about one o'clock.'

'Very well.' Amelia moved towards the door. 'I think I'd better go and start clearing my room.' Already her pulse was racing, her mouth dry.

'Melly,' Emma's tone was almost conciliatory, 'I like your dress, that apricot colour suits you. And the new hair style too. I always said you could do something for yourself if you made the effort.'

'Yes,' Amelia nodded wryly, 'you always did,' and retreated upstairs wishing that she could stay there until it was time to return to London.

Her small bedroom was clean and tidy and the bed had been made up. Slipping off her dress, she put on an overall from her case and went down the back staircase to ask one of the gardeners to bring her trunk up from the store room.

The rest of the morning passed too swiftly as she packed her books, pictures and oddments and sorted out what remained of her meagre wardrobe. She worked methodically, fighting against panic, knowing that there was no hope of avoiding Donovan Lyne; afraid of his displeasure when she wanted love; afraid of reviving the craving and foolish dreams she had managed to repress for so long. But there was no escape from the fact that she had behaved impulsively and very childishly and owed him an apology. And no matter how annoyed he might have been, she reflected, reassuring herself, he didn't really care; so contacting her was probably just a polite gesture.

Gradually she regained her composure. By the

time she had had a wash and put on her dress again, she was ready to face him. Standing in front of the mirror as she renewed her make-up and brushed her hair into soft, shining waves, she was relieved to see that although she was very pale there was no sign of the agitation she had been feeling. The thick frames of her spectacles added the final touch of camouflage.

Nevertheless, when the old grandfather clock in the hall chimed the hour a wave of apprehension swept over her. Without giving herself time for hesitation she went out on to the landing.

Donovan Lyne was already in the hall, talking to Edward, one hand on the newel post at the foot of the staircase: the same long, sinewy figure with its taut stillness, dressed informally in a brown turtle-necked sweater and tan slacks. Somehow the informality made him seem less formidable as she walked down the stairs confront him. But then he turned and their glances met and the smouldering look in his eyes made her heart contract. For an instant she stood petrified with shock. She had never seen such a harsh expression on his face, and she clutched the banister to prevent herself from running upstairs again.

Edward cleared his throat uncomfortably and came towards her. 'Amelia! Sorry I wasn't here when you arrived. Glad to see you, old girl,' he wrung her hand cordially, 'we must have a chat later. You two going in to lunch now? All laid on. Just give Haskins the nod when you're ready.'

He smiled at them both and disappeared, rather hastily she thought, in the direction of the kitchen.

116

'So!' said the abrasive voice, 'I've caught up with you at last.'

Refusing to look at him, because she was afraid of that harsh, inimical expression, she stammered, 'How —how are you?' and proffered her ice-cold hand uncertainly.

'Quite fit, thanks.' He ignored her hand.

'The fever——'

'I didn't come down here to discuss my health.'

Flicked on the raw by his arrogant, domineering manner, she found the urge to make amends deserted her. She looked up at his furious face, her eyes completely blank behind her spectacles, and said stonily: 'Why *did* you come?'

'What the hell have you been doing?' he snapped in a sharp undertone.

'Working in London—if it's of any interest.'

'I know that now, no thanks to you. And if you don't consider your wellbeing is of interest to me, you've become remarkably stupid in the last few weeks. Couldn't you have phoned or written a line to keep in touch?'

Tears welled to her eyes and she hurriedly averted her head and shoulders. He caught her by the arm and swivelled her round, none too gently. 'Don't turn your back on me,' he bit out nastily, 'you won't get far giving me the brush-off this time!'

'This time?' She swallowed her tears and compressed her lips until she could speak again. After a moment she said in a strangled voice: 'I had no intention of giving you the brush-off, as you put it, Professor. When you gave me that very generous cheque

I assumed that that was your way of trying to tell me you didn't need me any more at the flat. You had already made it clear that your secretarial staff at the Institute would cope with the rest of the work on the book. Then with Bill and Polly Austin coming to help you out there didn't seem much point in staying...'

'So you marched off into the blue, with no more than a few trite words on a bit of paper, before I'd had time to finish my breakfast!' His eyes blazed. 'For God's sake, Amelia, we knew each other better than that!'

A group of people came in through the front door, laughing and talking, stared at the arrested tension of the couple by the stairs and went towards the door of the club lounge. Donovan released his merciless grip on Amelia's arm and she leaned against the newel post, knowing that she would have to sit down soon or her legs would fail her. In all her expectations of meeting him again she had never foreseen such a flame of anger shrivelling her mind and heart. She was in a nightmare.

He continued savagely, 'It's irrational, I suppose, to blame you for escaping as soon as you could! But I would have thought it was common courtesy to let me know that you had somewhere to go, that you'd fixed yourself up with another job.'

'I hadn't, not at that stage,' she admitted huskily, rubbing her arm where she could still feel the bruising pressure of his fingers. 'I knew you wanted me to come back to Whimpleford, and I had no intention of doing so! I had to make a decision some time, and it seemed the right moment to get out of your way and find some other work.'

'Get out of my way? You mean get away from me!' he cut in caustically. He stared down into the pinched defencelessness of her face and said in a goaded voice: 'Hallow had no business to bully you into looking after me!'

'He didn't. All he did was to ask if I could cope, and I insisted that I could. You ... you needed help,' she faltered, prodding up her spectacles.

'But neither he nor I had any right to expect it from you. He was under a misconception about you and me. I wanted to talk it over, but I was too weak at first, and afterwards—well, there were other factors. How much did you resent it, Amelia? You were about as forthcoming as a clam.'

He broke off as another crowd of weekenders came streaming in. 'This place is like a zoo!' He swore impatiently. 'I wouldn't have chosen to meet you here, but there was no other way of pinning you down.' He put a hand under her elbow, and the renewed touch brought her emotions surging back.

'Let's go in to lunch.' He steered her into the club lounge. To her relief most of the members had gone through to the bar, and they found a quiet corner furthest from the door. While he ordered a couple of dry Martinis Amelia sank dazedly into a low chair with the window behind her, so that when he returned and sat opposite her the light fell across his features. He still looked angry, but much more controlled. His hair seemed greyer at the temples and the small lines more heavily marked in his face. There

119

had been nothing debilitated about his rage, nor the sheer force of nervous vitality. But the bout of fever had obviously left its traces. Seeing those deeper, bone-drawn lines filled Amelia with remorse, knowing they indicated the degree of stress to which she had thoughtlessly and selfishly added when his physical condition was low.

'Professor,' she leaned forward pleadingly, 'I didn't in the least resent having to look after you, please believe me.'

He seemed to get a grip on himself with an effort and said shortly, 'But for some reason you resented your hard-earned cheque. Why?'

'It was a kind of dismissal.' She looked up and met his compelling glance, then turned away, saying almost inaudibly: 'Wasn't it?'

He took the two glasses from the waiter and put one on the table near her hand. 'No, it was by way of an offer to release you from your distasteful task ... and the drudgery around the flat.' As he gazed at her bowed head his steely anger slowly evaporated. 'As a matter of fact I hoped you would go back with Bill and Polly that afternoon, Amelia. I thought Polly would be able to cosset you for a while to make up for the trouble I'd caused. Then back to Whimpleford to put a few things together, and off for a holiday before we found you a new job. I wanted to explain this when I handed over the cheque, but you weren't prepared to listen, were you?'

He was speaking quite calmly now, but it was a taut unnatural calm. He took a drink, shifted about restlessly. Constraint began to creep over them; that crippling alienation which had cut her off from him in the flat.

He said: 'I thought I might broach it later, before Polly arrived, and get Polly to persuade you to take a break. You appeared so deathly tired and—mute. When you vanished, I told Polly you'd come back here. As far as I knew you had nowhere else to go.'

Amelia raised her gentle eyes, overwhelmed with contrition, yearning to reach out to him and beg him to forgive her, but the look she encountered was bleak and austere. The complete change of mood in such a short time was as bewildering and painful as his anger. She sat up stiffly, biting her lip.

'I booked into a hotel and went to an employment bureau,' she said. 'I was fortunate, it worked out very well. Now I've been lucky enough to find a place in the apartment of a nice couple in the City.'

'And you're settling down happily?'

'Yes,' she asserted mendaciously, and looked pointedly away to where Haskins was hovering near the door.

'Good,' he said abruptly, nodding at Haskins and getting to his feet. 'Shall we have some lunch? You haven't touched your drink, bring it in with you.' He was towering over her in the chair, and she stood up quickly to avoid taking the long, square-tipped fingers extended to assist her.

He moved aside. Before stooping for her glass she forced herself to say coolly, tonelessly, 'Professor, about my leaving like that—I must apologise. I'm truly sorry. I was hasty and inconsiderate.'

'That conscience of yours,' he mocked, 'stirring

again?' Then with terse formality: 'No, Amelia, I should do the apologising. I was the cause of pitching you into a damnable situation, and I've exacerbated it by letting my confounded temper get out of hand. It was unforgivable.'

She made a small deprecating gesture and picked up her glass. There was a brief awkward silence. Miserably aware of him, she was afraid he would be able to sense it. They were so close, almost touching, yet further apart than they had ever been. His eyes went over her in a dispassionate appraisal of her new hair-style, her clothes, that hurt more than criticism.

'London,' he observed cynically, 'seems to have claimed you already.'

Fingers tight around the stem of her glass, she preceded him into the dining room, head held high, wondering how she would get through lunch.

As they made their choice of *hors d'oeuvres* he broke the crushing silence between them by asking casually: 'It *was* you I saw that night on the crossing at Holborn? With a man—a friend?'

'Yes, with Max Hall,' she owned with reluctance. 'The nephew of the people I work with now.' She went on to tell him about Hannah and Charles, stifling her wretchedness with words, frequently mentioning Max because she had to acknowledge his help. Donovan opened his mouth, as if to comment, then closed it in an inflexible line.

They ordered steak and salad and he chose a wine. From then on they talked like mere acquaintances, blandly polite. He brought her up to date on the progress on his book and inquired about her job with the visiting American. He ate sparingly, and Amelia thought every mouthful would choke her.

In the end the conversation became quite impersonal, as if their year together, the enforced intimacy of his flat, and the shock of his extraordinary outburst of rage had never been. They were discussing the weather prospects for the remainder of the weekend—it had come to that.

Looking over the cheese board, while she swallowed some fruit and cream with difficulty, he said in a preoccupied way, 'It's so mild and sunny I think I'll stay over until tomorrow. Relax a bit, a round of golf perhaps. Your brother-in-law tells me you're returning tomorrow evening. May I give you a lift back to town?'

'Thank you.' She looked up. Suddenly she remembered and the colour surged into her face. Carefully she adjusted her spectacles. 'It's very kind of you, Professor, but Max Hall will be coming down in the car to fetch me. If I'd known——'

'That's all right,' he interposed brusquely. 'No problem if you've already made arrangements.'

Had he given her a single breath of encouragement she would have gone straight to the telephone and called Max to cancel his trip. In spite of her misery she could not bear the thought of parting like this. She tried to say something, hoping for a miracle to restore their old amity, but he seemed totally indifferent now, and they finished their disastrous lunch in another oppressive silence.

She made the excuse that she was in the midst of packing and left him in the hall. She was glad neither

CHAPTER NINE

AFTER Donovan Lyne's abrupt visit to the Manor House, and her herculean effort to look cool and unperturbed during the rest of her stay, it took Amelia some days to settle down to the London routine again.

When Max had arrived at Whimpleford he had quickly spotted the change in her thin, oval face, and with surprising ease he had managed to lighten the pressures for her by charming Emma out of her malicious mood, and coping buoyantly with Edward's tiresomely bogus geniality. As they said goodbye in the hall, Emma had commented to Amelia in an arch undertone: 'So that's why you deserted Professor Lyne! You might have said so in the first place, but you never admit to anything, do you, Melly! Not that I blame you, Max is very attractive and much younger than that rude man! No wonder he was so put out!' Amelia had tightened her lips but had let it pass; Emma could think as she liked, for it would be a long time before she visited the Manor House with its unhappy associations again. Speeding out of Whimpleford, Max had thrown her a swift glance or two.

'The weekend wasn't a success, right?'

'No—I mean, yes, you're right.'

'You missed me, I knew you would!' he asserted with an impish grin, and plunged into a spate of light conversation which required very little response from her and was a blessed relief.

As she sensibly came to terms with the fact that Donovan Lyne had ceased, irrevocably, to have any part in her life, Amelia turned more and more to Max with a kind of resigned gratitude for which she despised herself, knowing that she was not being entirely fair in using him to salve her lacerated spirits.

She found herself drifting along on the tide of his sedulous attentions, going out with him to theatres, parties and noisily crowded discotheques, spending a reckless amount on deliciously feminine party clothes. She even changed her spectacle frames to please him. Her gentle manners amused and delighted Max after the aggressive worldliness of his other girl-friends and her innate reserve intrigued him. He rather fancied himself as Pygmalion, bringing her slowly to life.

Conquests had always come easily; Amelia presented something of a challenge, but Max was confident that she would surrender to him before long. The thought of marriage had seldom entered into his lighthearted approach to life, but he was more than half in love with her and the pull of sexual attraction grew, on his side, stronger every day. Amelia allowed him to kiss her. It was totally meaningless and she was quite passive. Then one evening, piqued by her unresponsiveness, he stormed her mouth with penetrating force and attempted to caress her. Amelia immediately recoiled and thrust him off so violently that he staggered back.

'Don't ever try that again, Max!' Her voice was obdurate, her eyes sparkling with outrage.

'For God's sake!' he said with baffled impatience. 'Overdoing the virtuous bit, aren't you? After all I've done for you I thought——'

'Well, you were wrong!' she retorted sharply.

How could she tell him of the sudden surge of revulsion which had shot through her?—or explain the fervent sense of belonging to someone else that still obsessed her? She turned away and added bitingly, 'Just don't take me for granted, that's all.'

'No need to snap my head off!' he exclaimed sulkily. 'I can't figure you out. One minute you're leading me on, giving in as docile as a lamb, the next you're spitting like a tigress.'

'Max, if you knew me at all well you'd know that I'm not really very tractable. I've been letting you have your own way in small things because ... well, because it was easier, and pleasant too.'

'Thanks,' he said sourly.

His discomfiture was almost comical, and he had been so good to her that she relented to a certain extent. 'All right,' she conceded, 'it was probably my fault it got out of hand. I'm grateful for the way you've helped me. But if we're to continue being friends you must understand that I'll only go as far as *I* want.'

'Okay,' throwing her a rueful glance, 'so I rushed you, and I'm all kinds of a clown, but one of these days you *will* want, and you can bet your sweet life I'll be around.'

127

She met his eyes squarely. 'No. I like you, Max —that's as far as it goes. Or ever will.'

His gaze narrowed. A few moments of silence, and he shrugged. 'There's a pretty tough streak behind that calm little poker-face, isn't there? Well, we live and learn.' Turning on his heel, he left her abruptly.

With the realisation of how distasteful any advances but Donovan's would be, Amelia wondered if the time would ever come when she could bring herself to surrender wholly to some other man. Perhaps some day—but not to Max. She would have to stop relying on him, and after this it should be easier to break their close personal contact.

She had not reckoned on his resilient spirit. The next morning his head came round the door of the small alcove she occupied behind the outer office. 'Pax?' he inquired hopefully with such an irrepressible twinkle in his eye that she weakened and then capitulated, nodding at him.

'I've got two tickets for the Haymarket theatre on Saturday. An Oscar Wilde revival, you'll find it amusing. Coming?' He slanted a grin at her. 'If I promise to be a good lad?'

She shook off her weight of oppression and smiled her acceptance.

The performance was not due to begin until after eight, and Max took her to dinner at a little Italian restaurant first. Amelia wore sapphire blue crêpe georgette, her hair brushed into a cap of shining waves, a light silvery stole over her shoulders with handbag and shoes to match. Max was a model of attentive but correct behaviour, and had put on a dark suit and plain tie as if to impress her in his new role of sober escort; but the wit and elegance of Oscar Wilde's play soon had them laughing, and by the time they went out to the dress-circle bar for a drink he had regained his ebullience.

She was waiting in the crush for him to return with the drinks when a voice beside her cried: '*Amelia!* It can't be! Good heavens!' and found herself confronted by the flushed face and sparkling hazel eyes of Polly Austin. For a second Amelia's mind went blank as her eyes tried to focus on the people behind Polly, looking instinctively for Donovan Lyne, but to her mingled disappointment and relief he was nowhere to be seen.

'Amelia, I scarcely recognised you ... oh, dear! ... I mean, you look wonderful. Fancy meeting you, out of the blue like this! Donovan told us you'd come up to town and found a new job, but he was so cagey about it——' She broke off, clasped Amelia's hand: 'Well! Why haven't you been in touch, my dear? I had so hoped we were going to be friends.'

Amelia's momentary embarrassment melted in a rush of warmth towards this eager, kindly little woman. 'Oh, Polly, it's so good to see you. I ... I did want to contact you, but—' *But I couldn't risk meeting Donovan* had to remain unspoken. Instead she finished lamely, 'I didn't want to impose on you after such a short acquaintance.'

'Impose, fiddlesticks! Even if Bill and I hadn't taken such a liking to you, the way you looked after

129

Don when he was ill practically makes you a member of the family! He told us how splendidly you managed without bothering anyone else, and if you hadn't had to go back to Whimpleford so unexpectedly Bill and I would have had a chance to thank you personally too.' Polly glanced away from Amelia's heightened colour and asked casually, 'Are you here with Don tonight?'

'No,' she replied, her colour receding. Just then Max appeared, shouldering his way through with two glasses held high for safety. 'Oh, Max, there you are. Polly, this is Max Hall—Mrs Austin.'

Max handed her a glass and turned his battery of charm on Polly. 'I leave one beautiful woman and come back to two! Mrs Austin, this is a great pleasure. May I get you a drink?'

Polly looked from Amelia to Max's handsome, rangy form and her face fell. 'Thank you, but my husband is bringing me one.' She tried to cover her dismay by plunging on chattily, brightly, 'Now tell me all about yourself—Max, isn't it? Do call me Polly. Amelia and I haven't met for some time, so I must catch up on all her friends. Bill, come and meet Max Hall.'

Bill Austin joined them, as balding and benign as ever, and the conversation continued almost exclusively between Max, cheerful and impudent, and Polly, doing her best to hide her hostility. Amelia sipped her drink and Bill watched his wife with a faint gleam of amusement.

Polly was so transparent, Amelia sighed inwardly.

To her she was still 'Don's Amelia' and Max Hall was trespassing. The bell rang, the crowd moved. Max took Amelia's arm possessively. 'I hope we meet again, Mrs Austin. You too, sir,' he said with polite deference to the age gap which brought a wry quirk of humour to Bill Austin's mouth as he set down their glasses.

'Indeed we must!' Polly cast a silent appeal to her husband. 'Bill, the party for Jean! Amelia, we'd love you to come!' A pause. 'And you, Max.'

'Of course,' Bill spoke equably. He caught the precipitate withdrawal in Amelia's eyes and asserted himself with surprising firmness. 'A friend of ours, married to an American, is over here for a few weeks and Polly has organised a dinner party at the Oberon Room, next Friday before Jean leaves for Los Angeles. She's a delightful person. You should meet her, Amelia.' He added astutely; 'Her husband is a writer, and as they have a wide circle of friends she probably knows of other Americans who need the kind of literary research I believe you're doing now.'

It was a shrewd move. Max's business instincts were immediately alerted to the advantage of the Hall agency, and he accepted with alacrity while Amelia stood by wordless. Polly was beaming at her and there was nothing Amelia could do without hurting her feelings. The likelihood that Donovan would also be there hung on her, half joy, half dread, as arrangements were made while they went into the auditorium.

Once they were in their own seats, Amelia closed

her eyes. 'Oh, Max,' she murmured, 'I wish—I wish we hadn't accepted.'

'Why not?' he returned, blithely unaware of the reason for her painful reluctance. 'It may be boring, but we can put up with it for one evening. More contacts, more clients, right? Lucky you knew them.'

All week Amelia worked obsessively on research for Harry B. Barnes, and by Friday morning she had virtually completed all the investigations he had given her. Work had so far held at bay the strained expectancy of seeing Don again, although she knew he would keep a polite distance after what had happened. She sank her head on her hands and mused dolefully on what Polly's reaction was going to be once she became aware of the complete estrangement between them. Dear Polly, so incurably romantic, so impulsive, so ... so *mistaken* in her affectionate concern for Donovan Lyne's interests...

Hannah Hall came in, and Amelia lifted her head and schooled her expression, and it was Hannah who said: 'Tired, Amelia? You've been working so hard you deserve some time off. It's the Austins' party today, isn't it? Why not take a break? Relax, have a hair-do and a manicure. Nothing like a bit of personal pampering to set oneself up. Off you go!'

So Amelia spent a few hours luxuriating in the lush, scented atmosphere of a salon; then, in another defiant gesture of extravagance, went into a small, exclusive gown-shop on her way home and bought a dinner dress in jade-green silk chiffon with a high, finely-tucked bodice and frosty lace at the throat and wrists. She hung it up where she could see it and sat for a long time in the familiar comfort of her grandmother's old rocking chair, slowly reasoning herself into equanimity. The evening had to be faced; it was likely, though not certain, that Donovan would be there. And if Polly Austin insisted on keeping up a friendship it was inevitable that Amelia would meet him from time to time. She must learn to behave naturally, drawing on all her resources of pride and common sense to see her through.

After a refreshing shower Amelia rubbed some of her favourite cologne into her skin, slipped into soft silk lingerie and carefully made up her face. The new dress slid over her shoulders, rounded her breasts and floated in gentle folds down to her ankles. When she crossed to the mirror to put the finishing touches to her hair she gasped a little at the transformation. A cool, soignée stranger stared back at her.

Max's voice could be heard from the parlour. Amelia swept up her stole and evening bag and joined them, feeling vaguely self-conscious at Max's uninhibited wolf-whistle and the compliments of the Clarks. Max looked handsomely trendy himself in a white silk polo-necked shirt with his black dinner jacket. He gave her an exaggerated bow of homage as he ushered her out to the car. 'You've done me proud, sweetie! Take my word, Miss Amelia Leigh will go like a bomb with the stuffed shirts tonight! I looked up this guy Austin; why didn't you tell me he was an egghead with the Fenn Foundation? Connected with that professor you worked for? You've got to keep up with the contacts, Amelia; never know what it'll lead to.'

She said uneasily: 'Max, they're friends. Don't— don't embarrass them.'

He got in beside her. 'Discretion,' he tapped the side of his nose, 'is my middle name.' He winked at her and switched on the ignition.

The red and gold foyer of the Oberon was bathed in light from a magnificent crystal chandelier, and the air was heavy with the scent of flowers banked around. Walking over the opulent pile of the carpet to the lounge Amelia ran her tongue over her lips, her mouth suddenly dry, and felt grateful for Max's hand under her elbow. The lounge was a semi-circular room furnished in Regency style with gilt and old-rose suites arranged in small, separate groups, some already occupied. Branches of pink-shaded candelabra softened the formality with a roseate glow, and glasses chinked against a buzz of conversation and laughter.

'Oh, Amelia my dear!' Polly, swathed in floral crêpe-de-chine quite unsuited to her plump figure, came to meet them followed by her husband. 'How lovely you look,' she said warmly, then with the slightest stiffening and change in manner: 'Ah yes ... Max, how are you? Nice to see you again.'

Max caught the tone and threw Amelia a quizzical glance, but Bill Austin intervened with a welcoming handclasp. 'What'll you have to drink?'

As he passed on their choice to a hovering waiter, Polly led them to where a man and a woman were sitting together. The man rose and Amelia's fluttering pulse subsided. It was not Don, but the broad, pleasantly ugly face of a stranger. The woman seated on the narrow gilded sofa smiled at her and Polly said, 'Amelia, this is my sister-in-law, Marguerite, and her husband, Tom Anderson,' and the introductions went round.

So this was Marguerite! Donovan's first love—and only love? Amelia could almost feel that scrap of paper in her hand ... *Flowers for Marguerite*. With a stab of envy she looked at the woman in the misty yellow gown, her glossy black hair curling in little tendrils around a small face and large dark eyes. A fragile, bird-boned woman most men would want to cherish and protect. No wonder Donovan had felt he couldn't subject her to the strenuous life he led. Did seeing her still disturb Don—like the sweet torture she herself had felt? She came back to what Polly was saying. 'Would you like to leave your stole in the cloakroom? I'd come with you, but Jeanie and Don will be here in a minute. Margo, take Amelia, there's a dear.'

He *was* coming—as she had known he would. And partnering the guest of honour! With a fixed smile Amelia accompanied Marguerite across the lounge to the powder room. A neat, grey-haired attendant took her stole and she sank on to a seat in front of the mirrors and tucked the counterfoil into her purse. To give herself time she made a pretence of tidying her hair, only to find that her hands were rather unsteady.

Marguerite tilted her head and said with a roguish look: 'He's very good-looking, Amelia, your—friend, Max Hall. Mmm, working for him must be quite different from slaving for a hard taskmaster like Donovan!'

The coy innuendo was irritating. 'I wouldn't call working for Professor Lyne slaving. I enjoyed it very much. And I don't work for Max Hall, we're colleagues.' Firmly Amelia changed the subject. 'Do you have any children, Mrs Anderson?'

'I'm always called Margo by my friends.' She darted a smoky glance at Amelia's reflection in the mirror. 'No, I can't cope with children. My health, you know,' she pouted prettily. 'As a matter of fact I didn't know if I would feel up to this tonight, but I couldn't miss the chance of meeting you.' She meant it, and not as a compliment. She bent towards one of the mirrors and started to examine her piquant little face. 'I do look a bit washed out, don't I?' she observed, and took a lipstick from her purse.

Although she was retouching her lips carefully, Amelia had the impression that she was still studying her surreptitiously and felt a prickle of disquiet. Soft and kittenish she might be, but tiny claws could draw blood.

'Oh, Amelia, I admire a woman like you so much!' She flicked the lipstick down and capped it. 'So strong and capable. You must have had a dreadful time nursing Donovan through that last bout of fever—all on your own with him in the flat,' she emphasised sweetly.

Amelia gave her a direct look, and her dark eyes

136

gazed back, the irises as sharp as pinpoints. 'Tell me, is it true about Don?' Marguerite slid a pink tongue over shiny lips. 'You've been so—er—close to him, and talked to the doctor, so you would know.'

Amelia raised her brows, coolly questioning, and Marguerite leaned towards her and spoke in a low, husky tone against the subdued voices of other women in the room. 'I believe this fever he picked up is more serious than anyone admits. Polly says he'll probably be going back to Sarava instead of taking the top job at the Fenn Foundation. Why should he throw away a wonderful opportunity like that?— unless he's a very sick person and knows he hasn't long ...' Her voice faded significantly.

Amelia sucked in her breath, as if her throat had been squeezed tight for a second. Such a possibility had never occurred to her. Was this why he had made that businesslike proposal? A competent wife he could trust to look after him, no emotional up-heavals, a child of his own to fulfil his life until ... No!—her heart rebelled. She rose jerkily to her feet.

'I'm sure you're wrong.' She smoothed her skirt, deceptively calm. 'He made a quick recovery. If he decides to return to Sarava it will be because he prefers the field-work of anthropology to being cooped up in an office dealing with administration. He ... he values his freedom, Mrs Anderson.'

'He does indeed,' Marguerite's eyes narrowed, 'as I imagine we *both* have cause to know.' A fleeting glitter, very like spite, was shuttered behind her thin, bluish lids. She shrugged and said: 'I do hope you're right.' She became absorbed in her own face again.

'I'm such a peaky mortal—just a touch more blusher, do you think? I won't keep you a minute.'

Amelia waited, concealing her impatience, trying to shut her mind to the appalling notion Marguerite had implanted, and to the conviction that it had been done quite deliberately to upset her. Incredibly it seemed that the woman had been waiting for this chance, was even jealous of her perhaps. For what conceivable reason?—unless Polly had been romanticising.

Marguerite clicked her purse shut, turned and bestowed a creamy smile. 'That's a gorgeous dress, Amelia, and you wear glasses with such panache! Don't laugh at little me, but from what I'd heard I've always imagined you as—well—a trifle *grim*. It's wonderful what clothes can do for a girl!'

'Thank you,' Amelia interrupted with chilly insincerity. 'Shall we go?'

Donovan Lyne was already in the lounge, immaculately tailored in evening dress, twirling a glass restlessly in his long fingers as he stood talking to Max. Even at a distance he seemed to dominate the small group. He looked up as the two of them approached. Over the dark head of her companion his eyes caught Amelia's with a flash of brilliance that stopped her in her tracks. But this was not the bright blaze of anger of their last meeting, and she suddenly felt shy and disconcerted. Then he was smiling urbanely, and Marguerite fluttered towards him and hung on his arm.

Watching him greet her as indulgently as he would a child, putting his glass out of her reach and laughing, all the petty animosity drained out of Amelia. Although she refused to believe Marguerite's conjecture about his health, she knew that the shock of it had drastically altered her own attitude towards Donovan. Whether he loved her or not no longer mattered; pride no longer mattered. What mattered was that she loved him—that he had needed her and she had failed him. How could she make amends now?

She was hardly aware that he had detached himself from the others and clasped her hand. Something of the ache of compunction that filled her must have shown in her face, for his fingers tightened around hers and jolted her into the realisation that he was staring at her with a strange expression.

'Amelia?' he said deeply; the inflection almost dissolved her limbs.

She wondered if he could feel the erratic throb of the pulse at her wrist; it was irrelevant whether he could or not, since he could have read in her shadowed eyes what she would somehow have to put into words before long. As soon as she could speak to him privately and tell him with honesty. If he would listen to her ... if it wasn't too late ... oh, the enormity of that 'if', which meant her whole future now!

'My God,' he said softly with a wry grimace, 'you look as though you expect me to tear you apart again! I was an unmitigated brute to you at the Manor House, I know it, I had no right. There's no need for you to tremble like this.'

She longed to silence his mouth with hers; she put

her fingers on their clasped hands instead. 'No, you mustn't think that.' She sought his eyes once more. 'Don, I want to talk to you. It—it's important—to me anyway.'

'About your job,' thin lines of tension deepened around his mouth, 'or is the boy-friend becoming too importunate? Looking at you, I can't say I blame him. Is it advice to the lovelorn you need, or a dour, fatherly academic to protect you?'

Amelia winced and withdrew her hand, stung by the sardonic change of tone. 'Neither,' she said helplessly. Advice to the lovelorn! The irony pierced her with its exact truth. Right deduction, wrong man, she thought numbly.

He scanned her face, puzzled by a vulnerability she had seldom betrayed except under the weight of his anger that day at Whimpleford. 'I was being flippant, I'm sorry. Amelia, what is it? What's worrying you?'

She glimpsed the misty yellow gown, the large dark eyes watching them avidly. 'Later, Don—some time when you can spare me a few minutes ...'

'But not here,' he said as if something had dawned on him, 'not here.'

'Now then,' Marguerite demanded gaily, 'what are you whispering about? Don, it's too bad of you. Amelia hasn't met Jean, or had a drink yet!'

A vibrant rapport held them together for another few seconds, then he slowly turned and impelled Amelia into the group, pressing his hand into the small of her back and moving his fingers against her spine in a way that ran fire through her nerves. Bill

Austin proffered the dry sherry she had asked for; Max grinned at her and raised his glass in a silent toast, a knowing glint in his eye. The hand at her back tensed and fell away abruptly. The physical link was broken, leaving her exposed, and all her senses cried against it.

'Amelia, this is my aunt ... Jean Laski,' Donovan's voice had reverted to dead-level urbanity, 'on a brief holiday from Los Angeles.'

The slim, vivacious elderly woman sitting on the sofa, very elegant in black velvet and lustrous pearls, drew Amelia down beside her. Her wide, humorous eyes lifted at the corners. 'Matchless Amelia! Oh, yes, at my age I can say it straight out and get away with it. I scarcely recognised the lordly, tyrannical being I used to know, and I hear tell it's your doing! Honey, you've humanized Don after his spell among the savages. How come?'

Amelia flushed scarlet at the ripple of laughter, not daring to look at Donovan, and murmured an inadequate protest. Donovan remarked dryly: 'Those savages, as you call them, have better party manners than you have, my dear, highly-civilized Aunt.'

'Uh-huh!' she chuckled meaningly, and plunged into a lively discussion about delving into old documents, skilfully drawing Amelia out of her shell until she succumbed completely to the older woman's extrovert personality. She remembered Donovan telling her that he had only one living relative. And she was as magnetic as he was, for she soon had everyone enthralled. She sat like a queen holding court, thought Amelia, sipping her drink and listening to her, fascinated, as the conversation became general.

Max had come to lean over the gilt back of the sofa, contributing his buoyant wit, and when Jean Laski had ended a particularly funny anecdote with a flourish, he leaned his head against Amelia, convulsed with merriment. She was laughing too, so were they all. All except Donovan Lyne. He looked at Max, then at Amelia, a hard, enigmatic glance that made her shrink away from Max and stop laughing. What now——what had become of that unexpected understanding which had bemused her mind and heated her blood? *Don ... Don ...*

She was still meshed in the cold grey scrutiny when, in a lull in the conversation, Jean Laski slanted a mischievous smile from Donovan to Max.

'Well, young feller, is Amelia taking you in hand as my nephew's successor?' she teased in a clear drawl. 'No, I guess you're up to all the tricks already. Maybe you could teach her a thing or two at that.'

'Chance would be a fine thing!' he retorted with a blatant wink.

Donovan sharply averted his head. 'You're incorrigible, Jean,' he sounded off-hand and faintly amused. 'Perhaps it's just as well you're going back to Los Angeles.' He tossed back his drink and jabbed his cigarette out in the nearest ashtray.

Amelia gripped her hands tight on her purse, the lump in her throat effectively preventing her from making a light comment to relieve the sudden strain. Marguerite said with girlish facetiousness: 'Oh, Don,

don't scowl so—think of all the beautiful Saravan maidens *you* must have deserted!'

Amelia rose to her feet with some kind of blind urge to walk out as the others laughed again, but Bill Austin gently took her glass from her and nodded at Polly, who stood beside him looking cross.

'Shall we go in to dinner?' said Polly in a high, hostessy voice.

CHAPTER TEN

THEY went into the dining room through a pair of ornate double doors at the back of the lounge. There were a few dining tables around an oval dance floor, but for the most part guests were accommodated along a wide pillared balcony surrounding the room. Each alcove was divided from the next by shaded lights and an arrangement of indoor plants which gave a discreet illusion of privacy. A small dance orchestra had begun playing soft rhythmic music from a dais at the far end, and three or four couples were swaying moodily over the polished floor.

Polly, all smiles and unshakable determination, insisted that Amelia should sit between Donovan and Tom Anderson, and placed Max on the other side between Marguerite and Jean Laski. Although she did not have to face the cold inspection of Donovan's gaze, sitting next to him in a small space was a bitter-sweet distraction for Amelia. The black-clad arm, so near her own, brushed against her flimsy silk chiffon, and the close, hard muscle of the thigh against hers unnerved her.

The Oberon was appropriately renowned for its superb English cuisine and impeccable service. Thick, creamy oyster soup was followed by sirloin of beef, with roast potatoes and scalloped artichokes, accompanied by an excellent claret. Amelia joined in a discursive conversation with Tom Anderson. He was a quiet, agreeable man, but Amelia could sense that, like herself, only half his mind was engaged. The rest was occupied in keeping track of Marguerite, whose large dark eyes were responding coquettishly to Max's lighthearted sallies. She had the art of flirtation and was busy using it to provoke her husband. And Donovan, no doubt, thought Amelia.

Tom Anderson was the impassive type who could watch and accept, knowing that Marguerite would always need the security he could give her. But Donovan was too highly-strung and assertive to be a passive spectator. Was she set on baiting him? Jean's tactless suggestion that Amelia herself had been playing Max off against Don had already annoyed him; if Marguerite was trying to irritate him further she was succeeding, because Amelia could feel the tautness in every movement he made.

She glanced at Tom Anderson. As their eyes met he broke off his rambling conversation, and she said impulsively, 'Marguerite is very beautiful. Have you been married long?' and could have bitten her tongue out for her crassness.

'We were married twelve months after Donovan went out to Sarava,' he supplied laconically, as though Donovan's departure had been crucial.

Amelia stared down at the delicious orange syllabub which had been set before her, covering her wine-glass with her hand as the waiter offered a Sauternes to go with it. Her head was inclined to swim, and not only with the wines she had been drinking—it required a great effort to be serene and

145

sociable with her mind constantly reverting to that poignant moment of shock in the cloakroom and the transitory warmth in Donovan's eyes and touch.

Donovan had not exchanged a word with her at the table so far, but when Tom turned away to answer a question from Polly, he bent his head and said in a mocking undertone, 'Don't take Max Hall's apparent defection too much to heart. Marguerite is essentially feminine and relishes masculine attentions, but that's as far as it goes.'

'Max is an expert,' she said lightly. 'And most women enjoy attentions.'

'You too, Amelia? How much you've changed. I seem to remember mine were not welcome.'

'How can you say that?'—what attentions? she wondered sadly—'We never had that kind of relationship, Don.'

She picked up her spoon; the whipped cream and wine of the syllabub melted on her tongue. Against the noise of voices and cutlery and the beat of the music he spoke again, still low but with a harsher inflection.

'Is that why you refused to marry me? Had I known you were open to the preliminary gallantries Max Hall is so *expert* at, I might have made the effort. Then perhaps the attentions I was threatening you with would have been more acceptable.' Under the mockery he was distinctly testy.

He meant his rights as a husband; she knew it and could almost hear him promising he would not be 'too tiresome and inconsiderate'. Colour ran up into her pallid skin.

'I didn't feel threatened, Don.' She looked into his eyes, saw the grey pupils widen and felt breathless. 'Never with you.' She put her spoon down.

'Not even alone one particular morning?' sardonically. 'I think you did.'

'It wasn't like that!' She swallowed convulsively, remembering the intimacy of his bedroom. 'Don, I couldn't—I mean, I wanted to explain——'

'You wanted *out*, Amelia,' was the pithy rejoinder.

'No!' she had spoken loudly, sharply, out of the fullness of her heart.

Immersed in each other as they were, the sudden pause around them went unnoticed. He said tersely: 'This is a hell of a conversation for the dining table, but let's get one thing straight——'

'*Don!*' squealed the girlish voice from the other side. 'Poor Miss Leigh! You're bullying and scowling at her and she looks quite stricken. She's not your humble Girl Friday now, you know!'

Donovan turned an impenetrable glance on her and was about to say something—suave but forceful, Amelia felt sure—when Max heaped coals of fire by laughing derisively.

'I wouldn't take bets on our meek-looking Miss Leigh! Beware of the quiet, tenacious ones. When they take something into their heads, nothing will shake 'em! And when they blow their tops it's either hell—or——' he fetched a dramatically soulful sigh, 'it could be heaven if it went the right way.'

'Personal experience?' Jean drawled at him, highly amused.

'Mrs Laski, the day I get to first base—as you

Americans call it—I'll send you a report by satel-
lite!'

It was hard to combat his good-humoured im-
pudence, and Amelia had to smother her exasperation. The best way was to try and smile, toy with the
feather-light cheese soufflé in front of her, and listen
to the talk which Bill Austin had adroitly picked up
and steered to the subject of earth satellites, space
travel and life on other planets. Polly joined in, but
was looking vaguely upset. Amelia said nothing, and
in a few moments gave up the pretence of eating, only
too conscious of the rigid displeasure of the man beside her.

Had he really been hurt by her refusal to marry
him? It seemed too long ago now to matter. Between them, Marguerite and Max had nettled him
into speaking of it again. Watching them had re-
minded him of the circumstances of having to ask
Amelia to marry him. Forced by illness, he had had
to return to England, for medical treatment and to
write his book; then after a year's respite in the
country he had to resume his former life, and it had
become expedient to have a wife of his own to stand
between him and the love of his life, his friend's wife,
until he was ready to go back into exile.

Well, I'm ready to go into exile with him, Amelia
told herself fiercely. What if it is second best for
him—at least I can earn his affection, and affection is
the true basis for love, for living together, for mental
and physical unity that lasts. Lasts while he lives ...
Panic knotted itself inside her even as she pushed the
thought away into the recesses of her mind. Involun-

tarily she put her hand on his arm. The muscle tensed. He looked round, down at her hand, then searched her face. He must have misunderstood the appeal in her eyes.

He said, low-toned: 'I'm not offended, Amelia, and I didn't mean to offend you.' He shrugged, 'Apologising is becoming a habit with us,' and turned away. Amelia dropped her hand, momentarily defeated.

The table had been cleared; coffee and liqueurs were being served to the women, balloon glasses of brandy for the men. Bill Austin soon invited Jean to dance, Tom Anderson followed them determinedly on to the floor with Marguerite, and tucked her slight form into his arms in a clumsily possessive way that made her pull a pouting little grimace at him. Max leaned across, took Amelia's coffee cup away, then stood up and held out his hand, smiling.

Reluctantly Amelia went with him down the three shallow steps to the dance floor. She had danced many times with him before, gyrating in the current style or close together as they were now. But she was unconsciously stiff, and missed a step or two glancing at the table where Polly and Don had their heads together, Don smoking restlessly while they chatted.

'Wake up, Sleeping Beauty,' Max muttered in her ear, hugging her.

She said coolly: 'Haven't you played Prince Charming enough tonight?'

'Jealous of that pretty little pixie, Margo?'

'Why on earth should I be?'—*yes, yes, I am, because of Don.*

149

He tilted his head back and quizzed down at her with narrowed eyes.

'I'm beginning to get the picture. No good giving me that hoity-toity stare, sweetie, Uncle Max has seen a thing or two tonight. It's the big bold explorer, isn't it! Professor Lyne,' he mimicked her voice. 'Some desiccated old stick, I thought, more fool me! You may think you're in love with that arrogant devil, but I don't give up that easy. Let's see what he makes of this!' He gathered her in a crushing embrace, his hand sliding down to her hip as he nuzzled his face against her throat.

She exerted all the pressure she could against him. 'Stop it, Max,' she said in a low, frigid voice, 'or I shall make a scene. Let me go at once!'

He released her to a more decorous hold. 'I wish you luck,' he said sullenly, digging his fingers into her back. 'You won't find the autocratic Professor as easy to string along as I've been. Little Margo's had a go at him if I read her right. For damn all!— and she knows every move of the game, so what chance have you?' He concluded with a hint of malice: 'Maybe you've realised that already.'

Amelia thought the music would never stop, but she managed to retain her cool pose while they returned to the table. Donovan Lyne rose, his grey eyes granite-hard as he seated her. Max's behaviour had not gone unnoticed by him, and he showed it in a deadly formality. Rather desperately she started another desultory conversation with Tom Anderson the moment he resumed his seat, and was startled to feel long fingers descend on her shoulder as the band began another number. 'My dance, Amelia?'

Willingly she let herself be led forward, and when Donovan's arms encircled her for the first time she was too overcome to utter a word. He seemed equally constrained. He held her lightly at a polite distance, a small gap but as wide as a chasm. Tension built up between them, and just as Amelia reached the point of finding it unendurable a young couple bumped into them, knocking her against him. She closed her eyes for a second, hearing their murmured civilities. Then, as the couple moved away, Donovan caught her close and she was enveloped in the aura of his masculinity.

Amelia gave herself up to the joy of it completely, her heart thudding under her ribs. Pressed to his lean, compact body, oblivious of her surroundings, willing him to relax and respond, she whispered longingly: 'Don!'

He missed a step and his arms became rigid. After an aching pause he said in a clipped voice, 'For God's sake, Amelia, don't try me too far.'

'I don't understand . . .' she faltered.

'Nor do I. Is this part of a ploy to punish Max Hall for his transgressions and bring him to heel?' The grip of his fingers began to hurt. 'Don't use me, Amelia.'

'Use you?' she echoed uncomprehendingly.

'All evening. The hints about wanting to confide in me—the appealing looks—the sad little protestations about our non-existent relationship. And now, this. Clinging for dear life, as if you meant it.'

She took a difficult breath. 'I do . . . I do mean it.'

They had come to a virtual standstill. His mouth was compressed and his brows were furrowed incredulously. He said with a touch of impatience, 'Mean what, precisely?'

'Oh, God!' She was in a quandary and it was hard to think. 'How can I tell you here? It's too personal.' In the middle of a crowd, of all places, to have to commit herself without knowing what his reactions would be. 'Don, please let me meet you somewhere. Tomorrow—the next day. Anywhere ...'

Before he could answer Max loomed up behind him and breezily tapped his shoulder. 'Professor, sorry to cut in. There's a phone call for you on the desk in the foyer, one of your colleagues from the Foundation. Must be urgent, or they wouldn't bother you here.'

For a fraction of time Donovan hesitated. 'Thanks.' As his arms slacked away the anticlimax made Amelia feel slightly sick. Max insinuated himself between them. 'I'll take over, Professor.' Slanting a grin at her, he said deliberately: 'Come on, Amelia mine, let's kiss and make up!'

Donovan's face was an icy mask. 'The ploy,' he told her sarcastically, 'seems to have worked.' Turning on his heel, he threaded his way through the dancers and out of the room.

'What was that cryptic comment about?' Max began. 'Hey, Amelia ...' But she left him standing on the dance floor.

Blinking back tears of frustration, she sat quietly at the table and sipped a liqueur to still the trembling of her limbs, and Max soon gave up his attempts to placate her. Ten minutes later Donovan came back to the table, but not to stay; something had come up, he explained briskly. He was abstracted, casual in his apologies and goodbyes, as if his mind was on other, important things. He barely glanced at Amelia, and when Jean Laski called laughingly to him to make the effort and write to her he waved a sketchy acknowledgement without looking back.

The rest of the evening dragged on with Polly, mystified, doing her best to keep things going; and by the time a penitent Max had taken Amelia home she was more desperately unhappy than she had been for many weeks.

The news was on the radio next morning. Sitting at breakfast with the Clarks she heard the word 'Sarava', then a report of earth tremors and fears about the dormant volcano. Was this why Don had been called away in such a hurry last night? Muttering her excuses, she left the table and hastily put on her light topcoat and cloche hat, collected her handbag and set off for the office. Her mind was fretting over the news and when she arrived she looked so pale that Hannah thought she was ill.

'No. No, I'm all right. I should like to make one or two personal telephone calls, if that's all right with you.'

'Of course, my dear. Use the phone in the back room—more private.'

Feverishly Amelia looked up Donovan's number at the flat, but there was no reply. Then she took her courage in both hands and dialled the Fenn Institute of Anthropology. It rang for quite a while, but as she was about to put the phone down, the switchboard answered.

She had to clear her throat. 'Professor Lyne, please.'

'One moment, please.' The silence weighed on her. She tried to think what she would say to him. The disembodied voice came back. 'I'm sorry, caller, Professor Lyne left by air for Sarava this morning.'

He had gone ... gone already, without giving her a chance ...

The sense of premonition that swept over her as she replaced the receiver left her feeling faint. Covering her face with her hands, she sat down heavily, convinced of disaster. He'll never come back, she thought—I'll never see him again—*what can I do*? Ring Polly—Bill Austin may be able to help.

'Amelia!' Polly's voice sounded tearful. 'I've been thinking of you and wondering——' She broke off. 'Don said he was sure the volcano would erupt. He's alerted the relief teams and gone off to see what he can do. As if he hasn't risked his life too often already,' she wailed.

The fact that Polly had jumped instantly to the conclusion that Amelia had phoned up about Donovan brought a lump to her throat, and her anxious voice made it worse. 'Amelia, are you still there? Amelia?'

'Yes, Polly. I tried to contact him at the Institute and they told me he had left, but I couldn't ask for any details.' Pausing, she said unsteadily: 'I don't know why I'm troubling you at a time like this, but I—I had to talk to someone.'

'Don't say things like that!—you know how close we are to Don, and how much we hoped, both Bill and I, that you and Don would get together. I could never understand what went wrong. You do love him, Amelia?'

'Yes, I love him, I always have.' It was a relief to admit it openly.

'Oh, Amelia, and I was sure he felt the same. What happened?'

She wavered for a few seconds. 'No, he—it's too complicated to explain now. If he ever comes back ...' Her voice thickened with tears and it took her a while to regain control. Sensing her distress, Polly rushed into a little spate of reassurances; how tough he was, how resourceful; how unforeseen his departure had been, which meant that he would have to come back as soon as he could. She was convincing herself too as she gave Amelia time to recover.

'Polly, I don't know anyone at the Institute, I can't pester them for news of Don. But Bill would know—I mean, Don will be in touch with him, won't he? Will I be a nuisance if I ring and ask you how he is and where he is?'

'Dear girl, we'll be glad to help, Bill knows you'll be as concerned as we are so you can phone us whenever you like.'

At the end of the conversation Amelia still felt very apprehensive, but not so alone.

The inevitable eruption of the Fire Mountain of Sarava made the headlines, and the force of its destructive power was an awesome sight in news films shown on television. Amelia worked, ate, and even slept with it in her dreams. The days dragged on. She and Polly commiserated with each other, but there was no comfort to be had; apart from a cable sent from Bali there was nothing new about Don because of a breakdown of communications with Sarava. Bill telephoned his contacts every day, without results.

Amelia had finished her researches for Harry B. Barnes, and as Hannah began to discuss finding her another assignment, she came to a momentous decision. She couldn't take any more. She was going to Sarava.

Both Hannah and Polly were horrified, although Polly could understand her desperation. Bill was noncommittal; in his practical way he could not see Amelia being allowed to visit the devastated area. She refused to listen to reason, or be put off, and suddenly remembered Dr Hallow, the one person who might be able to assist her, and was buoyed up with hope when he consented to give her a short interview in his consulting rooms.

He was brusque and forthright in his opinion of what he called her hare-brained scheme, but after listening to her earnest pleading he shot her a penetrating look from under beetling brows and said, 'All right, young woman. You've always seemed sensible to me, so I'll do what I can. Book your air fare to Bali. I'll arrange all the necessary inoculations for you and give you a letter to Dr Daud, an associate of mine out there. I can't promise you'll get any further than that. It will be up to you.'

She thanked him profusely, then paused and said hesitantly: 'Dr Hallow, is—is Professor Lyne's fever terminal? Please—please tell me the truth.'

'Who told you that?' She pressed a hand to her lips and he said, 'By rights I shouldn't discuss it with you, but in the circumstances—hmm! Frankly, it would have been, a few years ago. But there's a new drug to control the virus which will clear it up entirely.'

She stammered: 'You're not just s-saying that to——'

'Don't be foolish,' he snorted. 'Do you think I would have left you to cope with him alone if it was serious? He's getting it out of his system.'

At least one gnawing anxiety had been wiped away. Nevertheless, there was no dissuading her from her purpose. She might not be losing him through jungle fever, but the Fire Mountain was her enemy now, and she could not give Don up without a fight, without seeing him, being with him again ...

The Halls were solicitous. Max, surprisingly co-operative, volunteered to handle any further items Harry B. Barnes required; he appeared to have accepted the genuine depth of her feelings for Donovan Lyne. With Dr Hallow's help she soon obtained a visa, and was able to conclude all her preparations in a short time. She hurriedly bought some jeans and T-shirts, and a couple of long-sleeved blouses against the marauding insects of the tropics, and crammed her minimum needs into a small zipper suitcase. The Austins drove her to Heathrow. She was on her way.

It was a very long flight across the world. When

she left the transcontinental jet at Singapore the heat and humidity closed in on Amelia. Suffering jet-lag, she went doggedly on to the next stage of the journey with the blank singlemindedness of an automaton, boarding an Indonesian airline for Bali. At Denpasar airport a kindly official helped her find the telephone number of Dr Daud for whom Dr Hallow had given her a letter.

A woman's voice answered her inquiry, then, to Amelia's dismay, said: 'Dr Daud is gone to Sarava.'

'Oh, no!' Amelia was tired and confused. 'But I must see him!'

'You speak with Mr Kasir, the husband of his daughter.'

'Where?' Amelia wiped a trickle of perspiration off her throbbing temple with the back of her hand. 'Wait! Please say the number again ... slowly ... please ...' She fumbled in her bag for a pencil and scribbled it down on the back of the envelope for Dr Daud, paused a moment and dialled anew.

The final blow—Mr Kasir was out and would not be available until next morning. Amelia picked up her case, swaying uncertainly. She had to find a place to stay, to relax and sleep and restore her equilibrium. Approaching the kindly official, she asked him to direct her to a hotel.

'Much expensive, many *rupias*,' he said, eyeing her informal jeans and T-shirt and small suitcase. 'There is an inn, clean and fair price, not far.'

If she had any doubts about the suggestion, she had reached a point of not caring very much. He found her a taxi and gave directions in rapid dialect, and as they moved off she sat back limply, barely thinking.

Presently the taxi pulled up at a compound and she roused herself to get out and part with a thousand-rupia note for the fare. The night was humid and warm, the air smelt of incense and cooking spices and the sickly sweetness of a tropical creeper, but the rambling, unpretentious inn was much better than Amelia had dared to hope, of a type catering for tourists without much money to spare. The proprietor welcomed her with a beaming smile, and a few minutes later she was in a small, simply furnished room quite adequate for a short period.

A Balinese girl with a smooth, round, strangely beautiful face and wearing a brilliantly patterned *batik* sarong came to offer a *rijstafel* of various foods on a bed of rice, but the thought of food was nauseating, so Amelia settled for tea, and drank thirstily before preparing for bed. Checking through her money, she felt absurdly wealthy with so many thousand- and five-thousand-*rupia* notes until she recalled that it took hundreds to make a pound sterling. She hid the little hoard of notes and travellers' cheques and lay down.

What was ahead of her? she wondered wearily. Against her tightly shut eyelids she saw Donovan Lyne's face and was filled with foreboding. If she ever reached Sarava ... if she was permitted to go there ... would she find him? Alive? Her mind shied away from the alternative. Without him she might as well be dead too ... She began to drift into dreams with the weird sound of hammered chimes and gongs from a *gamelan* orchestra somewhere outside in the dark, scented distance.

When Amelia woke from a heavy sleep the sunlight was streaming in and her wrist watch showed it was almost eight o'clock. She washed and dressed quickly, her only thought to contact Mr Kasir. The proprietor of the inn arranged for her to use a telephone and she tried the number again in some trepidation. This time it was Mr Kasir himself. He spoke good English and she heaved a sigh and began a halting explanation, but although he was intrigued by her call he was not keen to have her visit him. Somewhat belatedly he agreed to come and see her at the inn; in about an hour, he said.

While she waited she breakfasted on fresh fruit and tea, seated on one of the cane chairs under the eaves of palm thatch, avoiding conversation with other visitors. For an hour and a half she lingered, looking at the sun-drenched colours of hibiscus, bougainvillaea and lilies in the compound, and was beginning to despair of Mr Kasir when a car drew up and a dapper, olive-skinned young man got out and approached her.

Amelia stood up, speculating on how much he would be able to do for her.

CHAPTER ELEVEN

'MADAME,' the young man bowed slightly. 'You are seeking Dr Daud?'

'Mr Kasir? Yes—I'm Amelia Leigh, from London. I have a letter for him from Dr Hallow, the specialist in tropical medicine. He knows Dr Daud well, and hoped that he would be able to help me.'

'Ah,' his rather solemn face widened in a smile. 'I also know this Dr Hallow, I have met him in London. You are a nurse wishing to visit Dr Daud? I regret he is not here. He has had to go to Sarava with a medical team in case of epidemics. He is an expert, like Dr Hallow.'

Amelia sat down and offered him a rattan chair near her. 'No, I'm not a nurse, Mr Kasir, but I want to go to Sarava too. Dr Hallow thought that Dr Daud might be able to use his influence to ... to get me there.'

He looked taken aback, then shook his head. 'Out of the question, madame! Even Dr Daud would not permit it. The area is very dangerous, and it is closed except to the medical and disaster workers at present.'

At the finality of his tone Amelia turned very pale. He leaned forward, his brow puckered. 'Madame, you are all right? You are not ill?'

'No, I'm not ill.' She straightened and faced him

calmly. 'I *must* go to Sarava—urgently—for personal reasons. If you can't help me——'

'I have not the power to do so,' he broke in worriedly.

'Then I will find some other way.' She rose, her disappointment hardening into determination. 'I'm sorry to have wasted your time, Mr Kasir.'

He stood up too, hesitating, concern and indecision in his expression: 'Have you a relative there? Nurse or missionary?'

'No.' A pause. She asked quietly: 'Do you know Professor Donovan Lyne?'

'Certainly!' He sounded awed. 'Is it to him you go?' He shuffled uneasily for a few seconds, then turned a troubled face. 'For Professor Lyne I will do what I can.' Seeing the sudden hope in her eyes he added hurriedly, 'It is not much, I cannot arrange anything, but if you will not say to anyone that it was from me, I will tell you how you may try and go there.'

He was eyeing her with renewed curiosity, and slight embarrassment, and it suddenly struck Amelia what he must be thinking. Her cheeks grew hot. If he thought she was Donovan's woman and was prepared to assist her, she was not going to enlighten him otherwise. 'I won't mention it to a soul!' she assured him. 'Not ... not even to Professor Lyne.'

'The professor is an important man. When all the trouble is passed there will be time to tell him I helped you. That may benefit me.'

'I'm sure he'll be grateful,' she said in a low voice,

162

then nearly laughed to see him glance all round like a conspirator.

'You must take the flight to Sumba Island. From Waingapu you can ride a bus to one of the villages on the coast. Then you may find a *prahu*, a sailing boat, that is willing to take you to Sarava. You will have to bribe them. You have money?'

'Yes—enough, I think. Please ... when can I leave?'

'If you are ready we can start now.'

Amelia fetched her case and paid her bill, surprised to find that her overnight stay had not cost her much more than the equivalent of a couple of pounds in English money. The beaming proprietor presented her with a spray of jasmine, 'our national flower', he informed her, inviting her to come again and tell her friends about the inn.

Mr Kasir first drove Amelia to change her travellers' cheques into *rupias*, wisely advising her that she would be needing cash and it would be difficult to exchange them once she was out in the countryside. Then he took her to the airport, imparting some more tips about managing on Sumba and a few common phrases of *Bahasa Indonesia* to use. He asked her to pay his respects to the great professor when the opportunity arose—but not a word to Dr Daud, who would be angry if he knew!

Amelia promised and thanked him sincerely, then said goodbye, almost sorry to see the last of his solemn face. She was alone once more, with the prospect of a difficult journey in strange places and no certainty of reaching Sarava. But at least she was better for a good night's sleep and had shaken off the utter helplessness which had beset her the evening before.

Checking flight times to Waingapu she found, to her consternation, that the two scheduled services left early in the morning. She had missed them for the day! She accepted this frustrating setback as calmly and sensibly as she could, and was preparing to return to the inn when she discovered that one of the flights had been changed at short notice. By hurrying through the formalities she was able to board it before take-off.

Some hours later she was at Waingapu on Sumba Island. The resources of this small place were being used to capacity by the relief services, and rather than risk being sent back she slipped out discreetly. Armed with the phrases she had jotted down phonetically from Mr Kasir, she made inquiries about buses, found a reasonably clean place for the night and kept out of sight for the rest of the long, hot, tropical evening. After eating a *nasi goreng* of chicken, vegetables and fried rice, with side dishes of chopped peanuts and sliced banana, she retired to her room.

The bus ride was the most uncomfortable and most colourful part of Amelia's unauthorised trek. She sat cramped in a babel of men, women and children, all brown-skinned and black-haired and bright-eyed, who shyly inspected her and smiled, then went back to their chatter of dialect. There were twice as many as the bus would normally hold, with chickens and a parrot to add to the clamour; and the rich, moist atmosphere reeked of perspiration, macassar oil, spices and over-ripe fruit. The bus lurched wildly over unmade roads from village to village. People struggled to get off and squeeze in. At one protracted stop Amelia had some tea, handed in to her through the window. Along another stretch a dispute started up in front and Amelia held her breath as the driver turned away from the wheel for endless moments to join in the argument; after which he switched on a radio at full blast, drowning everything in the drumming rhythms of native music.

Gradually the number of passengers dwindled until Amelia and an old woman were the only two left as the bus rattled to a stop near the coast. The driver looked at her as if he thought she was deranged, hoisted out her case and took the tip she offered with a grin. She watched as he turned the vehicle round and set off at great speed. The old woman had disappeared. Case in hand, trembling and stumbling a little, Amelia approached the sea.

The village was a daunting sight of dilapidated shacks and deserted lanes, littered with broken palm leaves. Nearer the beach she saw fallen trees, the exposed roots dangling with clods of dried mud, and when she reached the foreshore it was a bitter blow to see the mess of driftwood and damaged boats. There was a layer of fine dust on the battered palm trees and lumps of pumice bobbing and rolling in on the tide. And the gusty breeze filled her nostrils with a very faint but sickening smell of sulphur.

Fire Mountain! Amelia was frightened. Not only

were these the grim signs of the spreading ravages of the volcano far beyond the horizon, but the end of her foolhardy attempt to get there. What chance had she now of finding a boat? She stood very still, gazing out to sea, immobilised by the sheer futility of her efforts. Donovan ... Donovan ... she clung tenaciously to the thought of him; she would reach him somehow, whatever the cost.

Bracing herself to look round at the dispiriting prospects, she glimpsed some men moving about near two beached *prahus* further along the shore. She summoned her courage, but without much hope, and walked over and called out. They could not have been more surprised if she had dropped from the sky, and she was doing her best to make herself understood when a bearded sandy-haired young man appeared from behind one of the boats.

'Je-eez!' He stared in astonishment. 'Where have you sprung from?'

'Oh!' Amelia could have wept with relief. 'You're an Australian! Please will you help me ... please? I wanted to know if either of these boats is fit to sail. I—I want to go to Sarava.'

'You've got to be joking.' He looked dumbfounded.

'Ask them, please,' she insisted breathlessly. 'Say I'll pay well.'

'I don't need to ask them. This one,' he thumbed backwards, 'is mine. I got caught here on the tidal wave that flooded the coasts after the eruption, and it's taken me two weeks to get her into shape again.'

Amelia pushed up her spectacles and bestowed

her glowing smile on him. 'Then *you* could ... When,' she asked, 'when would you be ready?'

'I was planning tomorrow, the next day—when it suits me. But I don't reckon Sarava much, lady. Too dangerous!' She was at the end of her tether, and his woolly-bearded features blurred before her eyes. He said gruffly: 'Don't look so shattered. What do you want to go to that hell-hole for, and what are you doing out in the wilds on your own anyway?'

'Do you mind if I sit down?' She sank on to her suitcase and he squatted on his haunches beside her. The other men watched them before returning to work on their own *prahu*, the only one they had been able to salvage. Amelia pulled herself together and in a flat, tired voice recounted her story, which he pondered in silence. Bare except for scruffy briefs, the Australian looked none too prepossessing—nor do I, she thought, with my hair all over the place, crumpled jeans and a sweaty shirt and no make-up. His blunt, open manner seemed reliable enough. He probably thought she was an obstinately eccentric 'pommy'.

He got to his feet, scratched himself, and kicked aimlessly at the sand for a long minute while she sat waiting for him to make up his mind, then he said reluctantly: 'Okay, I must be as crazy as you are to agree to this! But if a chick like you can risk it, I'm willing. Tomorrow, if the weather holds, but no guarantees,' he threatened as she jumped up elatedly.

At that late stage they exchanged names; his was plain Sandy Smith, he said, and, 'I'll fetch you a bucket of water and you can sluice off back there among the trees. You can sleep on board tonight, I'll shack up in the village.' He wouldn't listen to her protests about putting him out, nor would he discuss taking money for the trip. Later, as they sat near the boat in eerie, sulphurous yellow moonlight, eating pannikins of boiled rice and vegetables, with prawn crackers called *krupak*, he told her he was a student on an island-hopping sailing holiday from Malaya back to Darwin. The villagers assumed she had come to join him and left them together.

'I still think you're crazy,' Sandy said. 'It was bad enough right here. Up the islands there was talk about earth tremors, but I wanted to push on and I was coming round the coast in the early hours of the morning when I heard the explosions. The last one was like an atom bomb—you could see the smoke on the horizon. By mid-morning it was pitch dark, raining ashes, sulphur and dust, and I switched to the engine and made for this bay. Then about an hour later the tidal wave hit us. Jee-eez!'

His sudden silence was more expressive than words. In spite of the warm, clammy air Amelia started to shiver uncontrollably.

'It's been quiet here since then. But what it's like on Sarava ...' He glanced at her huddled figure and said, 'Change your mind and go home.'

'N-no ... no,' she set her chattering teeth, 'I can face it, I *must*.'

'You really do go for this guy!' he commented, shaking his head. 'Come on, I'll get you up on deck and show you the cabin. You look knocked out.'

It was as poky and airless as a little box, cluttered

168

up with Sandy's gear, but she crawled gratefully on to the bunk and subsided as his hairy bare legs disappeared and she heard him go over the side. What am I doing? she asked herself dazedly, her mind a jumble of disorganised impressions. Would I have believed this a year ago in Whimpleford—or a month ago in London? How safe am I with this man? ... this stranger ... She fell asleep.

With the help of the villagers Sandy launched his boat next morning, and while he was busy Amelia gave them some money to ease their plight. After a meal of leathery, boiled sweet-corn they set sail on the afternoon tide. As the coastline dwindled behind them and the ocean swell took over, Amelia's stomach started to churn, something neither of them had anticipated, and to her mortification she was sick and had to retire to the cabin.

Sandy was a trifle impatient, then sighed philosophically. There was little he could do. She refused his offer of a drop of brandy and water with a shudder, and when he suggested turning back she pleaded against it with such a white, distraught face that he shrugged and returned to his tasks on deck. She lay, almost semi-conscious, through the long, hot hours of daylight. The cabin grew dimmer, but no cooler. Sandy came down and, removing her spectacles, wiped her face with a wet rag. Then he opened a tin of meat for himself and went back aloft. The cabin dissolved in darkness, and still Amelia lay on the smelly bunk, inert and uncaring.

A rough hand shaking her shoulder roused her sufficiently to sit upright, clutching her swimming head and groaning. 'What's happening?' she mumbled. 'What time is it?' Mercifully the dreadful pitching motion had ceased. She could hear the slap of water and a dull, intermittent rumble like thunder in the distance.

'Nearly dawn,' Sandy told her. 'You'll have to go ashore now, Amelia, it's the best I can do.'

'*Sarava*?' She could scarcely believe it, but it was enough to stimulate her senses. A lurid glow illumined the tiny cabin, and the stench of sulphur was overpowering. She put her feet down, scrabbled for her sandals and stood up. He grabbed her arm as she swayed. 'I hope you know what you're doing, mate, the more I see of it the crazier it gets. Roll up your jeans, we'll have to wade in. I'll take your case. Come when you're fit.'

A refreshing rub on face and arms with cologne from her handbag, a quick comb through her tangled hair; Amelia put on her spectacles, pulled out some money for Sandy and left it on his bunk to avoid arguments, then staggered up to the hatch and out on deck.

Sarava, at last. It was almost too much for her to take in at once.

They were in a small bay, in a sea of floating pumice. From the water line the beach curved like a burnt-out furnace of volcanic ash strewn with jagged chunks of rock and mangled tree-stumps, and behind this lay what must have been a tropical jungle, now changed into a desolation of ghostly trees withering under layers of dust. Amelia lifted her eyes to the blackened hills beyond, up along the remote ridges of the island to the blinding cone of Fire Mountain. A cloud of gas and dust still hung over the roaring cauldron of the crater from which streams of burning lava crawled down the sides, crumbling and spreading in fiery landslides of destruction.

The volcano rumbled ominously and Amelia shut her eyes against the terrifying sight. For a few seconds she panicked. Sandy put a hand on her arm and said, 'It's greasy getting ashore, the volcanic ash and water has turned into slime. But I had a look round before I woke you and there's a big camp on a plain back of those trees. Think you can make it?'

'I'll make it.' She set her teeth. Donovan would be there; that was all she cared about, all she could think about while Sandy wrung out a couple of rags in fresh water and instructed her to tie one over her nose and mouth. She slung her handbag round her neck and Sandy eased her slowly over the side. The water was shallow and warm, the pumice stones pelleted sharply at her bare legs. Somehow, clutching her sandals and his arm, she waded up to the beach and they stood for a moment looking at each other.

'Sandy,' she clasped his hand close, 'I don't know how to thank you.'

'Forget it! You're not much to look at, but you're a goer! Ready?'

'Yes ...' Taking her case, she asked, 'What will you do now?'

'Get the hell out of here! Go on, Amelia. Good luck, mate.'

When she reached the trees she turned and waved; he waved back and started wading out to the *prahu*.

Scrambling over a fallen tree, Amelia followed a well-defined path through the ghostly forest. Here deadness reigned; not a bird, not the smallest sound of wild life anywhere. It was so unnerving that when an indistinct call reached her on the heavy air she started to run, kicking up thick, loose ash with her heels, until she was out of the trees and on the edge of a large encampment of tents. There were two jeeps and a bulldozer on the far side, and a distant airstrip where the red morning glow was reflected on a helicopter and a light aircraft with Red Cross markings.

Light-headed with nausea, lack of food, and the thought of journey's end, she made for the nearest tent and stood faltering, dragging the mask away from her mouth and trying to push the words 'Anybody there?' through trembling lips. The tent flap opened, she had a cloudy impression of a white, buttoned shift, a broad pink face and a mass of gold hair twisted up in a knot. She heard a horrified exclamation, then blacked out in a sighing heap at the woman's feet.

Some time later she passed her tongue over her lips and made an effort to lift her eyelids. She was lying flat on a low camp bed. The sides of the small tent sloped up to a ridge-pole. There was someone in the tent with her, so she asked in a wavering voice: 'Can I have ... some water ...'

The golden-haired woman bent over her, raising her head and putting an aluminium mug to her lips. As Amelia drank thirstily, the china-blue eyes studied her face intently but not very sympathetically. Laying

172

her down, she put a hand to Amelia's forehead, pushed back her sticky hair, then took her pulse with the competent touch of a trained nurse.

'Do not be afraid,' she said quietly in English with a slightly guttural accent. 'The doctors have examined you. You have no disease or burns, only very exhausted just now.' She tucked a strand of flaxen hair into her bun. 'I am Lotte Meister. My husband is in charge of this disaster unit.'

Huskily Amelia gave her own name. The other nodded: 'I know. At first, when you appeared so mysteriously and quite collapsed, we thought you were another refugee—maybe from a mission, or some traveller stranded by the eruption. We searched your handbag for identity, you understand. There was this letter for Dr Daud, and he informs us that you have come from London.' After a short, rather pointed silence she asked: 'How have you found your way to us in such condition?'

'In Denpasar I hoped Dr Daud would arrange for me to get on to one of the flights,' Amelia sighed, 'but he had gone. So I went to Sumba instead and crossed over by sailing boat.' At the look in the saucer-blue eyes she rallied. 'I was all right, Mrs Meister. A bit seasick, that's all.'

Lotte Meister clicked her tongue, frowning, and shook her head. 'Dr Daud says you have come to contact Professor Lyne. If you are after a newspaper interview to make a sensation, I admire your spirit, but it will do you no good,' she said with some asperity. 'The press corps are all properly authorised here.'

'No!' Amelia hoisted herself up on her elbows. 'You mustn't think that!'

'Now, now,' Mrs Meister pushed her firmly back. 'What other reason or excuse?'

Amelia was past pretence. 'I love Donovan Lyne with all my heart, Mrs Meister. That's my only reason. To share this with him, be with him ...'

As she haltingly confided in Lotte, the other woman's face softened. 'I should not have questioned you until you were more rested.' She brushed the perspiration off her brow with the back of her hand, looking pensive. 'You should not be here, of course, but I begin to understand. My husband will have to decide this, and will do as he thinks best.' She moved away.

'Mrs Meister ...?' Amelia wiped a drop of moisture from her eye. 'I seem to have lost my spectacles ...' she whispered.

Lotte turned from the tent flap. 'On that folding chair beside you.'

'Do you think ...' Amelia fumbled to put them on, 'do you think I could see Professor Lyne?' She swallowed. 'Just for a few minutes.'

Her voice trailed into nothing and apprehension shot through her like a pain as Lotte Meister hesitated, glancing at her compassionately.

'No, not at present,' said Lotte matter-of-factly. 'He is not here.' Watching Amelia sink back and close her eyes, she continued in a bracing voice, 'He is wonderful, that man of yours. When we came first there was terrible confusion. It was he who could speak the various languages of the tribes and advised

174

us what should be done. And the lives he has saved —almost all! Without his special knowledge of this island there would be many dead who are now safe in the camp. He carries on his rescue work unceasingly. If it is possible he leaves markers for the helicopter, if not he sends the poor sufferers back by boat around the coast. Yesterday he radioed that he is searching another valley.' She came over and clasped Amelia's limp hand reassuringly. 'God will preserve the life of this brave man as he has preserved other lives, keep that thought to sustain you.'

Into the sudden pool of silence Amelia said in a quiet, resolute tone: 'Then I shall wait until he comes back, Mrs Meister—whatever the doctors say. I'm strong enough to work, I'll nurse, I'll do anything required. But I shall be here when he returns, however long it takes. Will you help me?'

'Such constancy?' said Lotte, smiling. 'Very well, I will do what I can.'

Amelia was ordered to spend the day resting, and was not summoned to the administration tent until the following morning. The knowledge that Donovan had radioed the camp less than forty-eight hours ago was a lifeline she clung to throughout the noisy, sweltering restlessness of the night. Lotte took her along the perimeter of the camp and showed her a dark, sheltered ravine where a small stream had survived practically unpolluted and was used by the womenfolk to bathe and launder their clothing as best they could. Amelia had a dip, put on her cleanest jeans and blue-flowered shirt and was ready, armed

175

with her inoculation certificate and other documents, when Lotte came to fetch her.

Feeling as guilty as any stowaway, she sat bolt upright in front of the medical officers. Dr Daud, a short, fleshy individual, asked her very briefly and politely about Dr Hallow, then bulged into a small camp chair and watched Amelia with large, brown, unblinking eyes. It was left to Dr Meister, as bald and sharp-nosed as an eagle, to pounce on her at every turn, trying to trap her like a rabbit with his questions before ramming home the tragic realities of the situation into which she had blundered. No time for imprudent escapades here, he implied, and no room for idle visitors. Just as Amelia began to feel she could not endure this lecture calmly for much longer, he picked up and looked through her papers.

He said grudgingly: 'Dr Hallow seems to have a good opinion of you.'

'Then let me stay and work, and prove it.' Her eyes pleaded quietly, and Lotte intervened for the first time to suggest that they could do with help in taking care of the orphaned children. She exchanged a look, a barely perceptible nod with her husband which indicated to Amelia that in spite of his stern attitude he had been aware of the whole story from Lotte already.

So began the hardest, longest days and nights of Amelia's life. At the camp there were twenty-five children in two large tents set aside for orphans rescued from the ravaged valleys of the island; most of them were unharmed, a few had minor burns, but all were bereft and in a state of shock which was heartbreaking. Amelia threw herself into the work, with a Swiss nurse and two native women, to get their emaciated brown bodies and terrified little minds fit enough to stand the journey by air to children's hospitals and homes elsewhere. She cajoled them to eat, cuddled them for comfort and encouraged them to relax by playing simple games, filling up all the set hours and more until she was ready to fall asleep on her feet.

She became used to the dust, the pervasive stench of sulphur, but the eroding horror of Fire Mountain was her bitterest enemy. Somewhere among those gaseous ravines and lurid trails of lava was a man, searching. Was he still searching? Was he still alive? The helicopter had made one flight in response to his call; then no more. And no more boats sailed into the adjacent bay. The doctors were always preoccupied; Amelia stopped asking them, masking her fears behind an impassive, white-faced exterior. Lotte said, without much conviction, that Donovan's radio must have failed.

Amela avoided the rest of the unit, the field hospital and big refugee camp; most of all the cameramen avid for anything that would make 'a story'. Every day, after the children's midday meal, when they had been put down to rest and she had hung up wet sheets to keep the dust and fumes out of the tents, she would wander down to the derelict beach to keep watch. And it was not until ten days of this hopeless vigil had passed that she saw the prow of a *prahu* nosing its way through the pumice towards the shore.

CHAPTER TWELVE

'DONOVAN ...' she mouthed soundlessly. And again in a high, piercing shriek: '*Don!*'

His head came up. 'Oh, my God!' he breathed, and stood still.

For an aeon they looked at each other across the littered desolation of the beach. Then he passed a hand over his eyes, smearing the sooty lines on his face, and the movement broke their stunned immobility. As he strode forward, Amelia started to run, tripping over the debris in her frenzied haste, blinded by tears pouring down her cheeks.

A charred, lacerated stump which had once been the living branch of a tree hit her foot and brought her down with a thud on her knees in ashy sand. Before she could fall flat he had caught her under the armpits and hauled her upright. Half-conscious, she felt the solid reality of his chest, the grip of his fingers, and the hard sinews of his thighs pressed against hers. The regular thud of his heart jarred into the core of her being, telling her he was alive ... alive!

Frantically she rubbed her hands over his arms, clung to his shoulders with a convulsive gesture, then reached up to grasp his hair as she strained to see his face through a blur of tears. His eyes, intensely brilliant in dark-ringed sockets, stared back incredulously.

She wanted reassurance—and more. She wanted, *needed* the certainty that he understood the compulsion driving her, and shared it. The turmoil of months of restraint and days of acute anxiety suddenly burst through the old barriers in an uncontrollable flood.

'How could you!' she raged, beating on his chest with tight fists. 'How could you do this to me! Have you any idea what I've been through? As soon as the earth tremors were reported on the news bulletin I knew ... I knew in my bones that you would go. Off to the ends of the earth, without so much as goodbye ... and not another word from you! What do you care about somebody else's private little hell?' She drew a shuddering breath. 'When we heard about the terrible eruption, Polly and Bill were almost as worried as I was. All the Institute could tell us was that you had sent a cable from Bali, and Sarava had no communications. Bill Austin did his best to get whatever news he could, but it was all about the gruesome conditions, never about you. It went on day after day, as if you'd ceased to exist. Don ... I nearly went out of my mind. I had to come ... I *had* to come myself! You could have been severely injured—or buried alive in this horrible mess—or dead —or dead!' she wailed, pounding out each broken syllable furiously on his chest.

'Amelia,' he said hoarsely, grabbing her wrists and holding her off. 'My God, I can't believe you're here. This isn't happening——'

'Isn't it?' she broke in wildly. 'Does it look as

though the sky's fallen in because it's me? Dull, un-emotional, boringly predictable Amelia!—have I up-set your precious notions of what to expect from me by chasing you out here and throwing a tantrum?' Her voice rose hysterically. 'You don't think I'm capable of feeling as deeply as other women, do you? Well, *I am*—but you've been too preoccupied and indifferent to notice.' She wrenched her wrists out of his grasp and shouted: 'Do you ever give a damn for those who love you, or consider the cost to them in sheer agony when you——'

A sharp whack across the cheek cut her short. She collapsed like a rag doll, and lay for a long time stifling her sobs against him while his hands moved roughly, possessively across her back. He said, 'I'm sorry I had to do that, but we have to pull ourselves together.'

Once the paroxysm of weeping had died down, Amelia took out a rag of handkerchief and blew her nose and dabbed the tears on her face.

'You did give me a shock,' he confessed with an attempt at normality. 'Getting out of the boat I felt so bone weary that when I saw you and heard your voice I thought I was having hallucinations! Then you exploded in my arms, and threw me right off balance.'

'Oh, Don, I don't know what's been happening to me,' she sniffed dolefully. 'I've bottled it up for so long that I couldn't help myself.'

'Too long,' he said huskily. Cupping her head, he tilted it up and stared into the bare, drowned look of her eyes. 'Amelia—dear God!—I can't take it in.

If only I'd known what was going on behind that calm little face of yours, I would have done this months ago,' and he brought his mouth down on hers in a moving, searching, sensual kiss under which she surrendered not only her lips but the whole fervent warmth of her body.

The ravages of Fire Mountain disappeared for timeless minutes as the two figures locked together on the beach appeased their craving for each other with a desperation intensified by their recent experiences. Don buried his face in the softness of her throat and muttered: 'Amelia ... love me ...', and his hands were hot on her skin under her thin cotton sweater as he reached up to coax and fondle and mould her body to his. Amelia arched her breast, oblivious of everything except the tumult of her senses, when he suddenly shifted, caught her by the arms and jerked her away. Dazedly she gazed up at him, as if shaken out of a deep sleep.

'No! ... no more!' He spoke gruffly. 'Help me to hold on, for God's sake. The conditions here have been so rough that the tensions have become unbearable, and there's a very thin line of control between us.'

'But if we love each other?' she whispered.

'Amelia,' he drew her to him and heaved a sigh over her upturned face. 'I can't get used to this—my prim, demure darling.' His lips brushed over hers lingeringly. 'You have no business to be here. This is no place——'

'While you're here, I'm staying with you,' she asserted vehemently.

His arms dropped. 'There's nothing left, nothing to stay for. Most of my tribe were blown to kingdom come in the first eruption; some of them who were cultivating their forest patches escaped only to be overcome by the fumes, and the remaining few were drowned in the tidal wave that followed. I rescued as many as I could from other tribes and got them to the camp. Since then I've been searching the ravines —it's all over.'

Compassion welled up in her for his extreme fatigue and his bleak acceptance that the tribe he had come to know so well had been lost. She put tremulous arms about his neck and drew his head down. 'But they'll never be forgotten, Don. They'll be there in your book, the way they lived and thought, and worshipped Fire Mountain. And those marvellous characters you met and recorded—they'll be alive for ever, my dearest.'

'Yes,' he conceded in a muffled tone, 'thank God I had enough time to complete that part of it.' Lifting his head, he said more firmly: 'I'll take you out of here—a few more hours. We'll try and get a plane to Waingapu tomorrow.' He rubbed a hard forefinger over the contours of her face and gave a throaty chuckle. 'You're streaked with soot and tears. And all those pink marks from my damned bristles,' he added ruefully, feeling his stubbled chin. He began to cough in a way that frightened her.

'Don!' She clutched at the remains of his shirt. 'Don, you're ill!'

'No, it's the results of the fumes, that's all,' he reassured her. 'My respirator gave out. I kept my nose

183

and mouth masked with a handkerchief for a while, but it gets through. I've got a bit of a sore throat, but it should clear up soon now.'

'Don, I must know the truth.' She strained closer and moaned: 'Don, I can't see you ...' She clapped her palms over her eyes. 'My spectacles, I've lost my spectacles!'

'Don't panic,' he gave another hoarse chuckle. 'They must have dropped when you fell over. Come on, we'll find them,' he said, and took her by the hand. 'Walk carefully.'

The spectacles were half buried near the signs of her fall close by on the beach, saved from being broken by the fine layer of white ash. Donovan blew on them and passed them to her to polish on her cotton sweater, remarking laconically that his shirt was too grubby. Amelia slid them on, and for the first time saw him clearly enough to be horrified. There were burn weals on his hands, his slacks were frayed and singed and his shirt full of holes and scorch marks. He shrugged off the shirt, rolled it into a ball and tossed it near the tree stump.

'Cinders,' he said casually, watching the anxious look on her face, 'it was pretty hot in a shirt, but it saved my skin from blistering.'

She went on staring at him; their glances were engrossed, telling each other with their eyes what they had whispered so incoherently together a few minutes before. She stretched out a hand and pressed it gently over the smooth brown skin and dark hair of his chest. 'I love you, Amelia,' he said unsteadily, clasping her hand and carrying it up to his lips to kiss her wrist and palm. 'We must be sensible, sweetheart. Wait here while I go and fetch my pack.'

He walked quickly away to the edge of the sea and picked up the small oilskin package he had flung out before climbing overboard. For a moment he stood watching the boat slowly disappearing around the island through heavy, pumice-strewn water; someone signalled with both arms from the stern and Donovan acknowledged it with a wave.

As he rejoined Amelia she could see how spent he was, and at the same time she marvelled at the stamina which had kept him going for days in the most appalling circumstances. What if he should succumb to another bout of jungle fever before they could get back to Dr Hallow? she thought worriedly.

She was filled with overwhelming love and solicitude which must have shown in her face, for he touched her cheek caressingly and said with a hint of wry amusement: 'For the love of heaven, don't look at me like that!'

'A cat may look at a king,' she retorted with a shaky laugh, the first genuine laughter for many unhappy weeks.

He smiled. 'Oh, I'm much humbler clay, my dear heart, an ordinary man with all the usual selfish needs and failings, as you'll soon find out. If there is one thing I know about you it's that you've never been catty to anyone, but if you really love me I shall feel like a king!'

She laughed again, tenderly, a tiny well-spring of joy bubbling up inside her. 'Haven't I proved I love you by coming here? And I'm willing to prove it still further in any way you want.'

'Anything?' His brows went up in mock astonishment.

'Ask, and you'll see.'

'Don't tempt me!' He caught her hand and turned her smartly around. 'Now, tell me how you got here. How long ago; and where have you been sheltering?'

So she told him as they strolled up the beach towards the forest path, their fingers closely entwined. 'Dr Hallow is a wonderful friend to you, Don. I wouldn't have been able to manage without his help, he has so many contacts through his work on tropical diseases. I've been sharing a tent with Lotte Meister and working with the children in the camp, trying to do whatever I could to help while I waited to find out what had become of you. Mrs Meister encouraged me to hope that you would come back, but they couldn't be sure, it was no use pretending ...' Her voice petered out and his hard fingers tightened around hers for a second or two in a grip that nearly made her cry out with the sweet pain of it.

'What shall we do now, Don?' she asked a little breathlessly as he vaulted the fallen tree and lifted her over. She rested against his bare chest briefly, savouring the moment.

'I'll go and report to the medical officers first. Then a good clean up,' he held her at arms' length and looked her over. 'You smell faintly sulphurous, like a witch.'

'Well!' she cried indignantly, 'that's a loving remark!'

His eyes glinted with laughter. 'You are a witch, you've been quietly weaving your insinuating spells around me for months. No, don't hide behind your spectacles, that little game is over for keeps!'

Busy and overworked though they were, the medical team hailed Donovan Lyne's return with sincere relief. He disappeared with Dr Meister and one of the officials into the office to have his burns tended and report on conditions on the other side of Sarava. Amelia had hung back while the others surrounded him, proud of their obvious admiration and respect for the eminent professor whose knowledge of the area and natural authority had been invaluable in the first chaotic days, and whose courage had helped them to save so many lives.

When he had gone Amelia turned towards the women's quarters to find Lotte Meister beside her lightly tapping her arm.

'He is a brave, good man,' she said kindly. 'You are happy again, and I am so happy for you too.'

'Yes ... yes ... thank you.' Amelia squeezed her hand and almost ran into the tent, dropping the flap behind her as the tears trickled down her cheeks. After a silent, emotional little weep she dried her eyes, put on her glasses and stooped over her small travelling case. She picked up her plastic wash-bag and cologne rub, and the pair of worn-looking jeans and long-sleeved blue-flowered shirt she had washed out the day before. Collecting her towel and undies, which had been hung on the tent ropes outside to dry, she went down to the forest pool.

The water was sluggish but cooler than the heavy

humid air, and she stripped and waded in, feeling it slide over her sweated skin, sighing with pleasure. She soaped herself lavishly, knowing that there would no longer be any need to eke it out, and even used a little to wash her hair. Drying herself hastily among the bushes, she massaged her skin with cooling cologne and got dressed.

Donovan loved her—somehow a miracle had occurred. She went over in her mind those revealing moments on the beach until her heart thudded against her ribs and her breath caught in her throat.

It was time for the children's evening meal. Amelia was sitting crosslegged on the ground, feeding a child as frail and tiny as a brown sparrow with small slow mouthfuls of milky gruel, when she sensed that Don had come into the tent. 'Gentle hands—I remember!' he said softly, and her pulses leapt at the sound of his voice. He had shaved and his hair was wet. He wore rather crumpled khaki slacks and a bush shirt and although his eyes had a sunken look he was very much himself again. *Because of me!* she realised with renewed amazement. No trace of that tired, dispirited man.

After the children had been settled for the night, they had their own frugal meal of some boiled rice and a mug of meat extract, swallowed their vitamin tablets, said good-night to the other workers in the mess tent and strolled out towards the ghostly forest again. Donovan put an arm about Amelia and held her close to his side.

She asked shyly, 'Where will you sleep tonight?'

'I have my survival pack. I can bivouac anywhere and sling up a hammock. Stay with me for a while?'

'For as long as you want me.'

He stopped and studied her pale oval features in the hazy, yellowish moonlight. 'Always,' he said soberly. 'There's a plane coming in with supplies from Waingapu tomorrow, and Dr Daud will get us out on the return flight. Then we'll go to Denpasar or Djakarta and on to Singapore. We can phone the Austins from there and let them know we're coming home together.'

Home together ... home together ... it was a benediction. High in the distance the crater of Fire Mountain smoked like a blazing cauldron with long glowing ribbons of orange and black lava. So beautiful—so lethal. Amelia shuddered. He caught her in his arms and lifted her face, kissing her until she forgot the awesome sight.

Presently he said huskily: 'For the second and last time—marry me?'

'Yes, of course—you know I will.'

'Do I? You turned me down pretty convincingly once!'

'That was different.' She drew away and stood a little apart. 'When you suddenly proposed you threw me into such a muddle!' She shrugged helplessly. 'I knew I was in love with you soon after we met, Don, but you gave no sign of thinking of me that way. You were stern and made me nervous ... talking about compatibility, and security, about not indulging in romantic nonsense. I felt so drab and inadequate—loving you so much, I c-couldn't accept.'

'God! I bungled it even more than I imagined!' His arms went round her, bringing the length of him hard against her back. 'It didn't take me long to discover the empathy between us either—and how very gentle and subdued you were. Over the months you became an essential part of my life.' He laid his cheek on her head. 'I loved you, wanted you, Amelia, but you were always so damnably reserved and self-possessed, as if you'd built a little wall around yourself with a No Trespassers sign! I couldn't gauge your feelings, and had no encouragement to show mine. One look from those calm, moss-brown eyes set me at a distance for days!'

She said diffidently, 'Was that why you never—well——'

He raised his head. 'Made a pass at you?' he supplied quizzically. 'Yes, you'll never know the discipline it took!—but I dared not risk losing you. I had to have you, my darling, on any terms. I thought that if I could get you away from the Manor House and all the unhappy associations, I might be able to awaken you and teach you to love me. I thought you would find it more acceptable if I made a practical proposition, not too demanding, and hoped that a child would bring us closer. And I had to give you the option of being rid of me if it hadn't worked out after a couple of years.'

'Oh, Don,' she struggled round and buried her face in his shoulder.

'Oh, Don!—is that all you can say after what

you've put me through?' he said tautly. 'You claim you were in love with me from the start, yet you behaved like a conscientious robot when I was ill! Do I sound rather—ungrateful? It seemed like the end when you walked out and left me flat because you didn't trust me.'

'No,' she quivered. 'I couldn't trust myself to stay ... I was miserable for weeks, and when you came down to the Manor House, so violently angry with me, nothing mattered any more—*nothing*. I even kept away from Polly for fear of meeting you. I couldn't bear you to look at me and treat me as though I were a stranger.'

'But the night of the dinner?—God! that's another world from this—You'd changed—something had changed. I could sense it, but Max Hall was around, and I thought you were trying to get back at me for my behaviour at the Manor House.'

'I *had* changed!' she retorted. 'It was something Marguerite said—it's not—it's not important now,' she put in hastily. 'But it made me see things differently, Don. I made up my mind that I'd marry you, if you would still have me—whether you loved me or not. And I longed to tell you. As for Max,' she moved with a little dismissive gesture, 'he's an amusing companion, I saw a lot of him, but I knew he could never mean anything to me. I belonged to you. He can be malicious sometimes, and he was a bit jealous that night ...'

'That made two of us! I wanted to kick him out of the place!'

She said in a muffled voice, 'I thought you were

191

furious with him over Marguerite.'

He stiffened. 'My dear, sweet idiot, where did you get hold of that idea?'

'Oh, just something I heard,' she murmured vaguely.

'That old story!' He groaned and went on wryly: 'When we were youngsters, Bill and I, we both protected her, took her around with us. Because she was Bill's sister, we were inevitably paired off, and it was flattering to show her off to my friends—the devoted little acolyte! So beautiful— beautiful and brainless. I was fond of her, I suppose, and people jumped to conclusions. But I had no intention of being tied down, and when it came to the choice between Sarava or Marguerite, I chose Sarava. Do you think I still have designs on Tom Anderson's wife?'

His arms tightened punishingly, crushing her ribs, making the blood pound in her throat. Marguerite and Max—and everything else—were irrelevancies while she stood in this bruising circle where she had yearned to be. Donovan raked his fingers through her hair and tugged her face up to his. 'To hell with the lot of them,' he said succinctly.

She had dreaded the thought that Sarava would separate them: instead it had brought them together. With a surge of happiness she gave herself up to the urgent possession of his lips.

There would be other rapturous moments of absolute surrender and intimacy with him, but Amelia would remember, for the rest of her life, how they had found each other in the shadow of Fire Mountain.